ATTACK OF THE VAMPIRE WEENIES

AND OTHER WARPED AND CREEPY TALES

STARSCAPE BOOKS BY DAVID LUBAR

Novels

Flip

Hidden Talents

True Talents

Nathan Abercrombie,
Accidental Zombie Series

My Rotten Life

Dead Guy Spy

Goop Soup

The Big Stink

Enter the Zombie

Story Collections

*The Battle of the Red Hot Pepper Weenies
and Other Warped and Creepy Tales*

*The Curse of the Campfire Weenies
and Other Warped and Creepy Tales*

*In the Land of the Lawn Weenies
and Other Warped and Creepy Tales*

*Invasion of the Road Weenies
and Other Warped and Creepy Tales*

ATTACK OF THE VAMPIRE WEENIES

AND OTHER WARPED AND CREEPY TALES

DAVID LUBAR

A TOM DOHERTY ASSOCIATES BOOK
NEW YORK

ATTACK OF THE VAMPIRE WEENIES
AND OTHER WARPED AND CREEPY TALES

"It's Only a Game" originally appeared in *Boys' Life*, May 2004.
"Lost and Found" originally appeared in *Orson Scott Card's Intergalactic Medicine Show*, October 2007.
"Get Out of Gym for Free" originally appeared in *Orson Scott Card's Intergalactic Medicine Show*, November 2009.

A Starscape Book
Published by Tom Doherty Associates, LLC
175 Fifth Avenue
New York, NY 10010

www.tor-forge.com

ISBN 978-0-7653-2345-3

First Edition: May 2011

Printed in April 2011 in the United States of America
by RR Donnelley, Harrisonburg, Virginia

0   9   8   7   6   5   4   3   2   1

For my dear friends Jim Vanecek, Ellen Riemschneider, Christopher, and Maryellen. Thanks for a lifetime of wonderful moments and fond memories.

CONTENTS

CONTENTS

ATTACK OF THE VAMPIRE WEENIES

AND OTHER WARPED AND CREEPY TALES

NOT ANOTHER WORD

I hate mimes. They're so annoying. Especially the one who's always doing his act in front of city hall. I see him on the way home from school every day. He's usually on the sidewalk at the bottom of the steps, performing stupid mime stuff like pretending to sit in an invisible chair or pulling a rope. Sometimes he's standing on the wide entrance area at the top of the steps, making fun of the way people walk.

"That guy is such a jerk," I told my friend Brayden as we turned the corner by city hall on a Monday afternoon. I'd never managed to catch the mime doing it, but I was sure he was always mocking me after I'd walked past him.

"I think mimes are kind of cool," Brayden said. "They're what clowns would be like if clowns weren't creepy. It takes a lot of skill to do those things."

"You've got to be kidding." I glared at the mime in his

stupid long-sleeved striped shirt, with his white gloves and painted face. "Anybody could do that stuff. Most people just don't want to humiliate themselves."

"You couldn't do it," Brayden said.

"Sure I could. Watch me." I walked toward the mime. As soon as he spotted me, he moonwalked past me, waving. Okay, I didn't know how to moonwalk, but I waited to see what he would do next.

He leaned over like he was resting his arm on a post or something. I did the same thing.

Then he stood up, bent forward, and acted like he was walking into a strong wind.

So did I.

I kept it up for a while. Whatever he did—I did the same thing. People started to watch us and laugh at him. Nobody tossed any money in his hat.

"Come on," Brayden said. "I'm tired of watching you make a fool out of yourself. Let's get out of here."

I bent toward him and whispered, "No way. I think I can get rid of him if I keep this up. I'll be doing everyone a favor."

"You're on your own," he said. "I'm going home."

"Fine. But you'll thank me tomorrow." I realized that this was my mission now. I was going to get rid of the mime. For good. Whatever he did, I'd do the same thing. After a while, I even managed to do a half-decent moonwalk. I was definitely giving him lots of reasons to leave. But I guess he was too stubborn to admit he'd lost.

Then I realized I had another weapon: Just because the mime couldn't talk, that didn't mean I had to keep silent. Whatever I was doing, I yelled it out in a totally obvious way.

"Hey, look at me! I'm trapped in an invisible cube!

"Whoa! I'm walking against the wind. Isn't that amazing?

"Oh, no! I have to carry this really heavy box."

Everyone who walked by stopped to laugh. I wasn't surprised. I had the sort of face that adults think is cute. It got me out of a lot of trouble. It was amazing the things I could get away with just by flashing a smile.

I'm pretty sure the mime didn't think I was cute. I kept waiting for him to get angry, but he didn't react to me at all for a while. Finally, after another half an hour or so of getting mocked and laughed at, he walked away from city hall with his shoulders slumped.

I followed him down the street. Sure enough, when he reached the next block, he put down his hat and started miming again. So I started mocking him again. I don't know why he thought a new location would make a difference.

He tried moving again a while later. And I followed him again. Nobody had given him a dime the whole time I was making fun of him. This was great. I promised myself I'd do this for as long as it took to get rid of him forever. I really hated mimes, and couldn't imagine why anyone would choose to spend his days like that.

"You've lost," I told him. "Find some other town. Go annoy some other people."

He didn't say anything to me, of course. But he obviously had no idea when to quit. He kept trying. I was getting tired and hungry. It was already past dinnertime. And it was growing dark. I figured he'd give up sooner or later.

Eventually, we reached the old bus station. It had been closed down last year after they built the new one, so there was nobody going past us. Nobody had any reason to be here. Even so, the mime kept doing his mime routine.

The streetlights flickered on. I looked around. There wasn't a single person in sight besides the mime and me. A slight tremor of fear rippled through my gut when I realized we were alone. But I was pretty big for my age, and I was a good runner. He wouldn't be able to hurt me. He wasn't a mugger or a gangster. He was a mime, which meant he was probably pretty much a wimp.

"There's nobody watching," I said while he pretended to reel in a big fish. "Give up."

He shrugged. "You win."

The words startled me. I figured he'd never talk.

He pulled a rag from his pocket and started wiping the thick makeup from his face. "You got what you wanted. You'll never see me again." His voice was deep but soft. Something about it made my nerves tingle.

"Great." I backed away a step. He was too calm. I'd trashed his whole act for hours, and he wasn't angry.

14

He looked at the rag, which was now covered with the white face paint. "SPF one thousand," he said.

"What?"

"Total sun protection. It's the only way I can go out during the day—with paint on my face and my lips firmly sealed, since the inside of my mouth is just as vulnerable as my skin. Oh, let's not forget the special protective lenses." He reached toward his eyes and popped something into his palm. His pupils were dark slits now. The whites of his eyes were shot through with blood vessels. His face was nearly as pale as the makeup he'd removed.

"I know my little hobby is silly, and not very sophisticated, but it is so very much better than spending all day in a coffin, waiting for the sun to set. And so perfect for finding the sort of victim that nobody will miss very much. People who hate mimes are often unpleasant and annoying creatures themselves. They are obnoxious little weasels who think they are important and superior."

He flashed a smile at me—but not the closed-lipped stupid mime smile he'd used all day. He opened his mouth for this smile, showing four long, sharp fangs. Vampire fangs.

In an eyeblink, before I could even turn away from him and start to run, he closed the distance between us and grabbed my shoulders in a crushing grip. He bent his head toward my neck. I could smell damp earth on his clothes and stale blood on his breath.

I opened my mouth to scream, but terror closed my throat and no sound came out.

"Who's the mime now?" he whispered as I thrashed in silence.

GET OUT OF GYM
FOR FREE

All right, you toads—line up!" Mr. Odzman screamed.

"What's he so angry about?" I asked.

"I heard he's always like that," my friend Curtis said.

"This is going to stink." I got in line in front of the bleachers with the rest of the class. It was the first period of the first day of middle school, and we had gym. I figured the gym teacher would be tough, but he looked like he was about to bite off someone's head and spit it onto the floor. Maybe after sucking out the eyeballs.

"I know what you worms are thinking," he said. "You're thinking gym is going to be awful. But you're wrong. It's going to be worse than awful."

He paused to stare at each of us, one by one. As his eyes met mine, I felt all my organs contract into fleshy spheres. Even my lungs constricted. For a moment, I couldn't remember how to breathe.

"But you're wrong about something else, too," he said. "It won't be bad for all of you. One of you is going to get a break. Whoever wins the free-for-all gets to skip gym for the whole year. Sound good?"

We all nodded. It's hard to nod and tremble at the same time.

"Free-for-all?" Curtis asked. "I wonder what the rules are?"

We found out a couple seconds later.

Mr. Odzman walked over to the door that led to the locker room. "Last man standing gets out of gym. I'll be back in ten minutes to see who the winner is."

He stepped through the opening and pulled the door closed. I heard a bolt slide into place.

Last man standing? I looked at Curtis. "He's got to be kidding."

There was something dangerous in his eyes. I leaped back as Curtis swung a fist at my head. His knuckles flew past my jaw. All around me, kids had exploded into action, punching or tackling whoever was nearest.

I didn't have time to watch any of that. Curtis staggered toward me, thrown off balance by his missed punch. Without thinking, I bent over and rammed my head into his stomach. He grunted and toppled over. I started to straighten up, but I felt a sharp pain in my back. Maybe using my head as a weapon wasn't the best idea.

Groaning at the pain, I straightened up all the way. Curtis managed to stand, too, but only briefly. Someone flew past me and tackled him. They both went down with a thud. I spun around, trying to spot any attackers.

The fight didn't last long. I got knocked down real hard from behind and twisted my knee. I couldn't get up.

Hiram Soames, who's been lifting weights since he was five and shaving since he was seven, won the battle. He was the only person standing when Mr. Odzman came back in.

"Very good," he told Hiram. "You get out of gym for the year. As for the rest of you, I'll see you next week. Unless you're too injured to come to class. You don't need a doctor's note. I'll take your word for it."

Too injured? I staggered to my feet and tried to take a step. I felt like someone was using my knee as a knife holder. My back ached, too. I had a feeling it would be weeks before I could walk without pain. All around me, kids were limping, groaning, and moaning. A couple of them were sobbing or whimpering. I saw a broken retainer, two nickels, three pennies, and a ripped pair of boxer shorts on the floor.

As we stumbled into the locker room, Mr. Odzman walked over to his office, dropped into his chair, and put his feet up on his desk.

"He looks pretty happy," I told Curtis.

Curtis glanced toward Mr. Odzman's office. "You'd be happy, too, if you didn't have to do any work."

"I guess so. I think we're all going to skip gym for a while." I headed for our next class. As I limped down the hallway and checked my schedule, a chilling thought hit me. "Curtis?"

"What?"

I pictured gas fires, powerful acids, toxic fumes, and broken glassware. "You don't think it will be like this in science class, do you?"

Curtis sighed. "I hope not."

I looked ahead of us, toward the science lab, where a plume of smoke poured out the door. Kids were crawling into the hallway, crying and moaning. One boy was stomping on his notebook to put out a fire. A girl raced past him, covered in dripping foam. Beyond them, through the doorway, I could see the teacher, wearing a pair of safety goggles and a grin.

It was going to be a long day.

GHOST IN THE WELL

Don't eat that," Mary said. "It will give you cramps."

Rachel studied the crab apple she'd plucked from a drooping branch of the half-dead tree. She'd heard the same warning ever since she was little. You weren't supposed to eat them. But she was starving. "My stomach already hurts. This can't make it any worse. I've never heard of anyone dying from a crab apple."

"That doesn't mean it hasn't happened," Mary said.

"Well, if it kills me, you can feel good about being right." Rachel bit into the small, hard fruit. The juice that trickled out was tart, like acid on her tongue. She chewed for a while before she swallowed. She opened her mouth for a second bite, then frowned and tossed the crab apple into a tangle of bushes behind the tree.

"You'll be sorry," Mary said.

"But at least I won't be hungry."

As they walked back to town, Rachel could swear she

felt the chewed-up piece of apple moving toward her stomach. She braced for sharp pains, but nothing came.

That night, as she was getting ready for bed, someone whispered her name.

Rachel opened the door and looked down the hallway. Nobody was there.

She slipped back into bed and closed her eyes.

"Rachel . . . help me. . . ."

She sat up and looked around. Then, feeling foolish, she spoke to the whisper. "Who are you?"

"Helen."

The whisper was firmer, clearer, as if her response had emboldened the speaker. *Helen?* Rachel didn't know anyone by that name.

"Where are you?"

"Outside."

"It's dark," Rachel said.

"You know your way."

Rachel walked to the hallway again. She checked to her left. Her parents' bedroom door was shut. There was no light spilling from the gap at the bottom. She got dressed, then sneaked out the back door, which, unlike the front one, never creaked.

She wondered what Helen looked like. The voice sounded young. But it's hard to tell with a whisper. Rachel peered all around. There was nobody in the yard.

"I don't see you."

"This way . . ."

She followed the voice toward the woods, and then down the path she'd walked with Mary. When the words led her to the crab apple tree, she wasn't surprised. Rachel looked up among the branches. She'd heard tales of wood nymphs from her grandmother.

"Are you up there?"

"No," Helen said. "Down here, behind the tree."

Rachel forced her way through the brush, then knelt on the other side of the tree. The ground was covered with dead leaves and fallen branches.

"Dig where the large root vanishes," Helen said.

Rachel stood up and looked back toward her home. Digging made her think of worms and other unpleasant things.

"Please," Helen said. "You're the only one who can help me."

"Promise you won't hurt me," Rachel said.

"I won't touch you," Helen said.

Rachel knelt and grabbed a handful of dead leaves. The work wasn't difficult in the chilly night air. The ground was soft and spongy. But still, she felt sweat start to bead on her forehead as she tossed aside the leaves and branches.

Eventually, unexpectedly, her hand broke through to emptiness. Rachel gasped and fought for balance.

"Careful!" Helen said after Rachel had steadied herself.

"What is this?" Rachel prodded at the springy mass of vegetation. She'd heard about people stumbling across the openings of caves, but not here in the woods. The caves she knew of were high up in the hills across the river, not hidden behind crab apple trees.

"An old well," Helen said.

"How—?" She wasn't sure of the right words to form the question. She pulled aside several more branches, but kept herself safely away from the expanding opening.

"I fell in," Helen said.

Rachel didn't understand how the opening could have gotten covered so quickly. She was sure Helen must be starving. At least, in a well, there should be water. "Have you been there long?"

"It feels like it," Helen said. "I couldn't really guess how long. Is Mr. Jefferson still our president?"

Rachel froze. Thomas Jefferson had been president right after John Adams, well more than two centuries ago. The broken branch in her hand suddenly felt far deader and drier than it had a moment ago. Minutes passed before she could speak again.

"That was a long time ago."

"I was afraid of that, but I knew it must be so," Helen said. "All the water has dried up."

"You're a ghost?"

"I fear I must be. I'm trapped here. Nobody has heard me until now. I need help."

The crab apple, Rachel thought. She looked at the roots of the tree. They'd grown deep into the ground near the well.

"Help me," Helen said.

A *ghost*. Rachel leaped to her feet and backed away from the opening. "I have to go home."

"No!" Helen yelled.

The force of the shout startled Rachel.

"Please," Helen said. "I need to return the gold bracelet. Then I'll be free."

"Bracelet?" Rachel asked.

"A beautiful gold bracelet with two diamonds and a ruby in it," Helen said. "Have you ever seen a ruby?"

"Never," Rachel said.

"They are so red, they almost seem alive. And the diamonds—oh, how they sparkled in the sunlight, like dancing rainbows."

"I'll bet they're beautiful." Rachel had seen small diamonds on other people's rings and necklaces. But she'd never even seen a ruby, or had a diamond she could call her own.

"Martha Vanderberg's father bought the bracelet for her," Helen said. "She boasted about it all the time, and about her fancy dresses. I didn't have anything. So I took it. It was wrong. I know that."

"Vanderberg . . . ," Rachel said. There was an old woman in town by that name. Gretchen Vanderberg. She was always talking about how her family had lived on this land for centuries. "I know that family."

"Then you can return the bracelet," Helen said. "I knew this was meant to be."

Rachel thought about the gold bracelet. She had to see

the diamonds and ruby. "I'll come back tomorrow. My uncle has a long ladder."

"No. You must do it now, while the bite of apple is still in you," Helen said. "After it is gone, you won't be able to hear me. Worse, I fear you won't remember me. You'll think all of this was a dream. It must be soon."

That seemed odd to Rachel, but no odder than talking with the ghost of a girl who had died so very long ago. What didn't seem odd was the bracelet. That seemed essential. She needed to hold it, maybe even wear it.

"How can I get it?" Rachel asked. "Can you toss it up to me?"

"I can't touch things. My hands pass through them. There's a barn nearby. Straight west of the tree. You'll find rope in there," Helen said.

Rachel didn't like the idea of stumbling deeper into the woods. "How do you know it's still there?"

"I can see beyond the well sometimes. Not far. And not always. But I know there's a barn and a rope. Be careful. The barn is old and the wood is rotten. I would hate to see you get hurt out there."

Rachel found the barn and the rope. When she returned, she tied one end of the rope around the crab apple tree, and dropped the other into the opening. "It's dark," she said.

"Not for me," Helen said. "I'll guide you."

Rachel knew she should turn and leave. But part of her needed to touch that bracelet. She grabbed the rope with both hands, tugged against the knot to be sure it

26

would hold her weight, then backed toward the opening of the well.

"Promise me you'll return the bracelet," Helen said.

"I'll see that the bracelet goes where it belongs," Rachel said. *Maybe it belongs with me,* she thought. Like Helen, she felt the world had given her less than she deserved. That was about to change. She could see the gold on her wrist already.

She took a step down into the well. And then another. The wall of the well felt solid enough. This would be easier than she'd thought.

The scream ripped through her ears like a thousand tortured voices exploding in her head. It hit so hard, it caused her real pain. Rachel slapped her hands over her ears.

It was a reflex. But a deadly one. As she fell, she clutched desperately for the rope in the blind darkness.

She missed.

It was a long fall.

"Hello," Helen said.

Rachel, too stunned to speak yet, looked at the girl. She was young, maybe ten or twelve, and pretty, with curly brown hair. Behind Helen, against the wall of the well, Rachel saw a small skeleton. She looked down and saw her own lifeless body. She quickly looked away.

"Why—?" Rachel's mind felt numb, like she was halfway caught in a deep sleep. Her body felt nothing at all.

"I've been terribly lonely," Helen said. "Until now."

"But the bracelet," Rachel said. "How can I return it? How can I help you be free?"

"Oh, there's no bracelet," Helen said. "That was a lie."

"A lie?" Rachel couldn't believe the beautiful ruby never existed.

"I'm very good at lying. That's why I was being chased by the other children. That's how I fell into the old well."

A touch of anger broke through Rachel's numbness. "Then how was I supposed to set you free?"

"I don't think there is a way," Helen said. "I suspect I'll be here forever. But not alone. Not now that I finally found someone to drop in and keep me company. So, tell me all about yourself, and about the world. Has much happened since Mr. Jefferson was elected?"

"I'm never speaking to you again." Rachel stared toward the top of the well, and toward the world she'd left. "You tricked me. You're a horrible person."

"Oh, you'll talk," Helen said. "Maybe not now. Maybe not for a day or a year. But sooner or later, you will. I can wait. I'm very good at that, too."

IT'f ONLY A GAME

Somewhere in Idaho . . .

Please, Dad," Lucas said. "Everyone else has the
Game-Jammer Channel. Can't we get it?"

"If everyone jumped off a bridge, would you jump?"
Lucas's dad asked.

"Yeah," Lucas said. "I mean—no." He realized there
was no safe answer to that question, so he stopped trying
to find one and went back to pleading. "Come on, I'm the
only kid in school who doesn't have a new system. All
I've got is your old Atari, and that's from the last century."

"It was good enough for me," his dad said with that
tone that meant *no more discussion.*

Lucas shook his head and stomped up to his room. It
wasn't fair. Every single one of his friends had the new
Game-Jammer Channel. They got games streamed into
their systems right off the cable—real games, with 3-D
worlds and awesome audio—while he was stuck with
that ancient machine. The resolution was so low, you

29

could see the pixels, and the sounds were a joke. Just beeps and buzzes. Half the time, the cartridges didn't even work unless you put them in just right or blew on them real hard to get the dust off.

Lucas plunked down on his bed and stared at the stupid old game. He felt like smashing it. Then his eyes wandered to the cable outlet on the wall.

Why not?

He unplugged the cable from the back of his TV, then looked at the game system. There was no cable socket. Lucas remembered something he'd seen in a box in the basement. He ran down and searched through the old parts. Yup, there it was, all the way at the bottom—a converter that changed a cable signal into an old-fashioned antenna wire. He also grabbed a signal splitter and some extra cables.

Lucas ran back upstairs and attached the converter to the game system and then used the splitter to attach the game to the TV. It was a tangled mess of wires and cables, but he figured something interesting might happen.

"Here goes." He switched on the power.

Somewhere between Mars and Jupiter . . .

"It is a rich planet, and it will soon be ours," Mexplatle said as he examined the data flowing into the bank of instruments on the panel in front of him.

"Excellent," Rubnupshti said, rubbing his noses together in glee. "Any sign that they will resist?"

"No." Mexplatle wagged his elbow. "Once we have landed and set up our shields, their primitive missiles and atomic weapons will not be a threat."

Before Mexplatle could say more, a warning flashed on his control panel. "Hang on to your fleexbriddle," he said. "We're heading for a field of asteroids."

Somewhere in Idaho . . .

"Unbelievable," Lucas said as the game came up. "This is cool." He grabbed the joystick and started playing. He'd never expected to actually get a game off the cable on the old system. But this looked great. There were asteroids all over the place, zooming toward him at high speed. The resolution seemed a little higher than on any of his dad's old games, but it was still pretty primitive.

"Wow, that was close." Lucas barely avoided the first huge rock. He got the feel of the game pretty quickly and started making his way through the obstacles.

Somewhere between Mars and Jupiter . . .

"Franzleglip!" Mexplatle swore, yanking on the controls with all his strength.

"What is wrong?" Rubnupshti asked.

"I'm not in control. We are doomed. The ship is flying itself." He closed his eye and folded his ears as an asteroid shot right past them, just missing the viewport.

"I knew I should have stayed home," Rubnupshti said.

Somewhere in Idaho . . .

"That was close," Lucas said. He'd barely avoided a collision as three asteroids crossed his path with only a narrow space in between. But he was getting through the game.

An hour later, he finally saw an end to the asteroid field. Six more big rocks to get past, and he'd be finished.

Two asteroids, side by side, came at him from the top of the screen. He just managed to fit between them. He angled to the left to get past the next three. There was only one more asteroid to go.

Somewhere between Mars and Jupiter . . .

"We've made it," Mexplatle said. "One more asteroid and we are past all danger. Then we can claim that planet for ourselves." He imagined all the wealth that awaited him. He'd be famous. He'd be rich. It was wonderful.

Somewhere in Idaho . . .

This is it, Lucas thought. The last asteroid didn't even look that tough. In a couple of seconds, he'd win the game.

"Lucas," his dad called from the hallway.

"What?" Lucas asked, not looking up.

"Sometimes I forget what it's like to be a kid. I've got a surprise for you."

Lucas glanced over. His dad was holding up a brand-new

video game system. "Wow!" Lucas dropped the ancient joystick and leaped up. "Can we get the Game-Jammer Channel, too?"

"Sure," his dad said.

Lucas glanced back at the old Atari. On the screen, his ship hit the asteroid and exploded into a billion pieces. Lucas shrugged. It didn't matter. The old machine didn't have very good graphics. He was sure the new games were a lot more realistic.

ATTACK OF THE VAMPIRE WEENIES

I ignored the doorbell. I knew who was out there. I knew what he wanted. It rang again.

"Get it, jerk!" my sister yelled from upstairs.

I'd rather chew on a lightbulb than turn that doorknob. But I didn't want Tammy angry with me. The last time she got really mad, she painted splash marks on the front of all my pants with clear nail polish, so it looked like I'd had an accident. The time before that, she'd e-mailed all my friends baby pictures of me getting a bath in the sink.

Hoping I was wrong about who was out there, I turned the knob, then opened the door halfway and stared up at the vampire. He wore a black cape with a red lining. His hair was slicked back so it glistened in the moonlight. His cheeks were pale white. Dark circles made his eyes look like they had sunk into his skull. He started to step into the hallway.

"You have to be invited," I said. "That's the rule."

34

He shoved the door, knocking me back. "Get lost, squirt."

"It's the rule!" I shouted as he pushed past me. "A vampire can't enter a home unless he's invited. Everyone knows that."

He walked over to the stairs and called up, "Hey, Tammy! I'm here. Come on. The party's already started."

"I'll be right down," she said.

Dalton—that's the name of my sister's boyfriend—went into the living room and plopped down on the couch.

I followed him. "You can't sit there."

He glared at me. "What's your problem?"

"It's not my problem, it's yours." I pointed at the small cross that hung on the wall between the photo of Grandma and the painting of a cactus my parents had bought last year when we were on vacation in Arizona. "Vampires can't stand the sight of a cross."

He leaned forward and put his hand on my shoulder. "Look, kid. I *am* a vampire. So don't tell me what I can and can't do. Just go read your comic books, or whatever it is that gives you all those ridiculous ideas."

"You're not a vampire," I said. "You're just a vampire wannabe. Wait—I know—you're a vampire weenie. That's what you are."

"What did you say?" His eyes got dangerous. For an instant, he almost looked like someone who could drain the blood from my body. "Come on—open that smart mouth again."

He sprang up from the couch. I took a step back.

Tammy drifted into the room. "Okay, I'm ready. Let's go."

Dalton seemed to forget I even existed. I guess he liked the way she looked.

I can't imagine how anyone—except maybe an undertaker—would feel that way. She was wearing a long white dress and too much makeup. The circles around her eyes were larger than his. Her cheeks were white, but with a touch of red. That was wrong, too. Vampire skin is as white and lifeless as the belly of a dead fish.

He touched her cheek. "You sparkle."

She touched his. "So do you."

They headed out.

"For crying out loud—vampires don't sparkle!" I shouted as the door closed. Okay, it was after the door closed. But I was angry now, and felt like yelling. "You aren't vampires. You're just big kids playing dress-up and acting moody. You don't know the rules, you stupid sparkly vampire wannabe weenies!"

I could feel my own blood boiling. Tammy and her friends were completely giggly and weird about vampires. They had vampire parties all the time, where they drank strawberry soda, cherry punch, and even tomato juice. They read books and watched movies where the vampire was always this unbelievably handsome guy. That was so totally wrong. They didn't know anything.

A vampire isn't some sort of handsome prince. And a vampire definitely isn't some gloomy teenager who flunked algebra twice and likes to pick on his girlfriend's little brother. A vampire isn't a girl who's read some stupid book seventeen times and thinks she can become one of the characters.

A vampire is a bloodsucking horror who sleeps in a coffin filled with his native soil; lives with bats, rats, and spiders; and carries nothing inside himself but death and disease. A vampire shies away from crosses and can't stand the odor of garlic. He needs permission to enter a house. Holy water burns his skin. He'll die if he's exposed to sunlight or if you drive a wooden stake through his heart. But even with a stake through his heart, he won't remain dead unless you chop off his head and stuff the neck with garlic.

Tammy and her friends would know this if they read the right books—the old books. But they'd rather dress up in silly costumes and drink fake blood than learn the truth.

My parents were out—they go out all the time—which meant I was alone in the house. That was fine with me. I went up to my room to play *Soldiers and Snipers*. I might know everything there is to know about vampires but, unlike Tammy, I had other interests, too. Like online multiplayer shooters.

I heard Tammy and Dalton when they came back late that evening.

"We should have the next party here," Tammy said.

"What about your parents?" Dalton asked.

"They'll be out of town next weekend," Tammy said.

I already knew about that. Dad was going to some sort of convention in Boston. Mom was tagging along, since seeing Boston was probably a lot more fun than staying home with her kids.

"What about your brother?" Dalton asked.

During the pause that followed his question, I felt a shiver dance across my skin.

"We can lock him in the basement or something," Tammy said.

Great. They were going to have a party with all their stupid vampire friends, and I'd get to sit in the dark on the basement stairs, listening to footsteps on the ceiling, waiting for them to let me out.

I stormed downstairs. "No way you're locking me in the basement."

Tammy almost looked guilty, but Dalton grinned. "We'll do whatever we want. You have no power over us, mortal. Begone, or I will unleash my fury upon you."

"Vampires don't grin, either," I said. "And I do have power: I'll tell my parents."

"You do and you're dead," Dalton said.

"Then I'll die happy." I stood my ground. I knew they had to give in. They wanted their party more than I wanted to escape a beating. "Look, I don't care about your stupid party. I won't even come downstairs. I'll stay in my room. But there's no way you're locking me up."

Dalton looked at Tammy. Tammy looked back at him. They both shrugged.

"Just keep out of the way," she said.

"That's exactly what I'm planning to do."

But as I headed back upstairs, I realized I wanted to do one other thing, too. If all Tammy's vampire weenie friends were coming to a vampire party, I was going to give them just what they were asking for.

The idea was so perfect, I froze on the steps when it hit me. Somehow, somewhere, I was going to find a real vampire and get him to come. That would teach them a lesson.

I knew vampires were real. I knew they were out there. There were too many myths and stories. Too many legends. There had to be a source for all of that.

And when the real vampire revealed his foul, evil nature, and all Tammy's friends were cowering and screaming, I'd step in with my vampire-killing tools and save the day.

That was such a great plan. I'd shut them up for good—and be a hero. Tammy would never be able to boss me around again. Dalton would tremble when I stared at him.

I just needed to find a vampire. I checked my books for ideas, but nothing I read seemed like it would help me lure a vampire to the party. Most people were much more interested in keeping them away. If knowledge wouldn't do the trick, I'd have to go with a guess. I was pretty sure about one thing—vampires must hate all the stuff people think about them. All that wrong stuff and nonsense.

That was it!

If Tammy and Dalton's endless babbling made me angry, think how furious it would make a vampire.

I typed up a flyer for the party. I made it sound so fannish and nauseating that no living person who saw the flyer would be tempted to come. But I also made it so extremely stupid in a vampire weenie sort of way that any real vampire who read it would be sure to come.

At the top, I put SUPER AWESOME VAMPIRE GET-TOGETHER. Below that, I wrote,

Come sparkle with us. Have oodles of dark fun playing vampire games and making new vampire pals. There will be bloodsicles, coffin cakes, and lots of other goodies.

I went on for a full page, tossing in every wrong thing I'd ever heard Tammy talk about, along with a bunch of stuff I made up. I finished with, *Your vampirific hosts, Tammy and Dalton, would like to fang you for coming.*

I ran off two hundred copies on my dad's printer and walked all over town, stuffing them where people would never go but vampires might—in crypts at the cemetery, behind the blood bank, and through the cracked basement windows of abandoned buildings.

I had a good feeling about my plan. It was going to work. I'd bet anything that a real vampire would come to the party, just to show the vampirific Tammy and Dalton how wrong they were.

Saturday evening, Tammy put on some creepy music and lit a bunch of candles. I don't know what candles had to do with vampires. They can see in nearly total darkness. While she and Dalton were out buying chips and stuff, I set up the room as a vampire trap. I hid the cross behind the picture of Grandma. I hung another cross behind a calendar on the other side of the room.

I chopped up a whole piece of garlic and put it inside one of those sealed plastic tubs that the wonton soup comes in when we have takeout. I washed the outside so it didn't smell at all and stuck the container under the couch, where I could grab it when I needed it, along with a couple wooden stakes. I kept the holy water in my pocket. I'd sneaked into Saint Sebastian's yesterday and swiped some. Just a little. But that's all I needed.

I waited upstairs, watching out the window. Tammy and Dalton's stupid vampire weenie friends started showing up right after sunset. The flyer said the party started at ten o'clock. I didn't want the vampire to show up until all the guests were here.

I'd know him when he came. He'd stop at the door to ask permission to enter. And those fools would give it to him. He'd probably hide his face somehow, since they'd never let him in if they saw how horrifying he was. They're so lucky I was planning to save them. Though, if the vampire started his feast with Dalton, I'd be tempted to hold off until he was finished.

I spotted the vampire when he was half a block away. It had to be him. He was taller than any of Tammy's friends, and he didn't move like someone rushing to a party. His head was down, so I couldn't see his face, but I could just imagine the horror of it. He was wearing dark clothes and a cape.

I sneaked out of my room and watched from the top of the steps.

The doorbell rang.

Tammy went and opened it.

"Oh my!" she said.

The room fell silent, as if the vampire's presence were enough to suck the sounds from the air.

"Whoa!"

That was me. I managed to choke back my gasp. It didn't matter. I don't think anyone would have looked in my direction even if I'd smacked the wall with a baseball bat. Not when they had *him* to stare at.

If you gathered the ten best-looking movie stars on the planet and squished all their good looks into one person, that person would look ugly next to the visitor at the door.

All the girls acted like they were about to faint. The man—I mean, the vampire—spoke.

"Good evening." He put his hand on his chest and bowed. "Count Vranski asks permission to enter this house. Who gives it?"

"You won't drink our blood, will you?" Tammy asked.

He smiled at her, and she let out a little whimper. "I would never dream of doing that," he said. Then he repeated the question. "Who gives Count Vranski permission to enter?"

"I do." Tammy took a step toward him. "Please come in."
"With pleasure." He moved into the room.

I couldn't believe how handsome he was. But he was still a vampire, and I was still going to save the day. Even if I was wrong about how he should look, I knew I was right about the rest of it. He'd go for blood, soon. And I'd be the hero.

Downstairs, all the kids had gathered around him. "So," he said, "you are not afraid of vampires?"

"We *are* vampires," Dalton said. "All of us."

"Perhaps some of you will be exactly what you think you are, soon," Count Vranski said. He stared at Tammy, locking his eyes on to her neck.

It was hero time. I leaped down the stairs, raced over to the picture of Grandma, and knocked it off the wall, revealing the first cross.

Then I ran to the other wall and pulled down the calendar.

"Trapped!" I shouted, reaching into my pocket for the holy water.

Instead of cringing or flinching, Count Vranski sighed and walked toward me. "You've been reading too many comic books, young man," he said.

"Back!" I shouted, holding up the bottle of holy water.

He plucked the bottle from my hand, unscrewed the cap, and drank the water.

"Ah, refreshing," he said. Then he walked over to the wall, took down the first cross, and slipped it into his pocket.

"You can't touch that!"

He answered me by pointing to the empty spot on the wall, then patting his pocket.

All the myths couldn't be wrong. I reached under the couch and grabbed the garlic. By then, he'd taken down the second cross.

I pulled back the lid and thrust the container at him.

He wrinkled his nose. "Pungent. It would make a good marinara sauce." Then he grabbed the container away from me. "We don't want to stink up this nice party."

I followed him into the kitchen. He dumped the garlic in the sink and ran it through the garbage disposal.

"Anything else you want to thrust at me?" he asked as he headed back toward the living room.

"No . . ." I'd lost. I felt like GAME OVER was flashing above my head in giant red letters. "That was everything I had." I couldn't believe my stupid sister and her vampire weenie wannabe friends were right.

"No stakes?"

"Oh, yeah. I forgot. They're under the couch."

He reached down and pulled out the stakes. "That's it?" he asked.

"Yup." I glanced at Tammy. I really didn't like her expression.

"Cheer up," Count Vranski said. "Pretty soon, you won't even care about what these people think."

I turned away. Then I spun back. "Wait!"

Count Vranski looked at me but didn't say anything.

"I'm not wrong. There's another explanation why none

of this worked on you." I pointed at him. "You're not a vampire!"

He shrugged. "I never said I was."

"Sure you did. When you came to the door. You said, 'Count Vranski asks permission to enter this house.'"

"And he does." He stared at me like he was waiting for me to figure something out.

My jaw dropped as the truth sank in. He'd never said he was Count Vranski. I looked past him. None of the kids had a clue. They were looking at me with the mocking expressions big kids always have when they think someone did something childish.

"They're ready for you," the man said.

He spoke quietly, but I knew the person he was talking to could hear him no matter how softly he whispered.

I spun toward the wall and reached out, forgetting for an instant that the cross was gone. Both of them were gone. So was the holy water and the garlic. I had no stakes to thrust at undead hearts.

The door flew open so hard, it shattered against the inside wall.

Someone old and evil and horribly ugly stepped into the house. His skin was dead white. His teeth were the dull brown color of old blood. A smell of rotten flesh and unwashed clothing drifted from him. White flecks wriggled in his hair and fell to his shoulders. Maggots.

He slithered over to Tammy. "Thank you for the invitation. I brought my friends."

Tammy screamed. So did all her vampire wannabe

friends. They tried to run out of the room, but more vampires burst in through the windows. I heard glass shattering all over the house. I guess once one of them was inside, he could invite the rest.

Count Vranski glanced over at the good-looking guy who'd tricked us. "Well done, Samuel," he said. "You may leave now. I know you need lots of sleep to help you keep those good looks."

"Yes, master," the man said. He bowed. Then he turned to me. "I told you this wouldn't matter for long. Enjoy the party."

He slipped out the door. I tried to escape, but someone grabbed me. A horrible face thrust toward my neck. The smell made me so sick, I hardly felt the bite.

He locked me in his grip as he started to drain my blood.

"I was right," I gasped.

Somehow, that didn't seem important anymore.

RAPT PUNZEL

Awhile ago—however long it actually was doesn't really matter—a poor couple lived in a shack in the woods. They had enough money for a television, but they couldn't afford cable. So they settled for watching the few shows they could catch on broadcast. When the wife learned she was going to have a baby, she got restless.

"Look there," she said, pointing to the high walls that surrounded the witch's home not far from their shack. "She has satellite TV. And all we have is broadcast."

"I'll fix that," her husband said. He waited until night, then took his tools and sneaked over to the satellite dish. He spliced a second cable into the line and ran it to his shack.

"Now we can watch everything," the husband said.

"Isn't that stealing?" the wife asked.

"We're not hurting anyone," the husband said.

And so they settled down on the couch and watched the wonderful abundance of available satellite programming while they waited for their daughter to be born. From the instant the baby girl, who they named Punzel, set eyes on the television, she was mesmerized. She spent every waking moment staring at the screen, totally rapt. So did her parents. At night, in her cradle, she fell asleep to the comforting glow of the screen and the lilting melody of talk show theme songs.

One evening, as the husband and wife sat on their couch, admiring their new baby and watching an ancient rerun of *Delaware Shore*, they heard a knock at their door.

It was the witch. She wasn't smiling.

"I didn't do it!" the husband shouted. As his scream bounced back at him from the walls of the shack, he realized he should have waited until he was accused of something before he started shouting denials.

"You stole my signal," the witch said as she strode over to the crib. "And now I shall steal your daughter. You're lucky I don't turn you into a newt. Or a minnow." The witch snatched the infant from her cradle and left.

She locked Punzel in a high tower with no exit except a small window. Punzel didn't care. There was a TV in the tower. The witch got three hundred channels. And it was a big TV. Really, really enormous.

Each day, Punzel watched her favorite programs and surfed the channels in search of new shows. Each evening, the witch flew up to the small window and visited

Punzel. Together, they would watch reality shows and make fun of the contestants.

Years passed. Punzel grew into a young lady. And her hair grew long and full. The witch never cut it. Punzel never asked for it to be cut. She was happy watching TV, enrapt by the images.

One day, a prince heard a rumor of a fair maiden trapped by a witch in a tower. He traveled through the woods until he found her.

"Punzel!" he called.

"Shhh! *Supermodel Showdown* is on," she said, not even looking over her shoulder. She'd seen this episode seven times, but she kept hoping the ending would change and the mean model would win. So far, no luck.

The prince wasn't easily dissuaded. He'd fought drag-ons and bested ogres. "Punzel, rapt Punzel, let down your hair," he called, "so I may climb the golden stair."

His timing was perfect. A commercial for a miracle hair-growth formula had just come on. Punzel certainly didn't need that. And she felt it would be nice to have some company other than the witch for a change. She grabbed an armful of her hair, which by now filled nearly half the room, and tossed it out the window.

The prince, watching from below as the hair cascaded from the window, was the first to suspect this may have been a bad suggestion on his part.

Had Punzel ever ventured into channels 245 through 267, where the science shows were stuck, she might have had a clue, herself, of the huge mistake she'd just made.

But as much as she knew about fashion, celebrities, and cakes, she was clueless about the basic laws of motion, force, and acceleration.

Alas, ignorance of the laws of science does not protect you from them. Her hair, all eighty pounds of it, along with another ten or twelve pounds of accumulated dust and debris, fell from the window until it was yanked to a stop, by her thick head. Which, unfortunately, was perched on top of her less-thick neck. Which, even more unfortunately, having been weakened by years of motionless viewing and a diet lacking in sufficient calcium, snapped like a stale bread stick.

"Punzel?" the prince called after the hair had stopped falling. "Are you hurt?" He didn't hold out much hope for an answer. Even from far below rapt Punzel's window, the sound of the snap was clear and loud enough to make him wince.

The prince left. The TV kept playing, even though nobody was watching it anymore. It didn't care.

IN ONE EAR

We get to listen to music during study hall, which is pretty cool. I have an MP3 player. So do most of the kids. For the whole period, we're all bobbing and bouncing and feeling the music. It's fun—you can tell who's listening to a fast song by the way he moves.

There was a new kid, Everet Meeps, who's really weird. He listened to music, like the rest of us, but he took his earphones out every five minutes or so. I didn't really pay much attention to him at first, but after a while, I couldn't help noticing him. He'd be listening to his player and studying, but then he'd put down his pencil, yank the earbuds out of his ears, and put them down on his desk. Then, a minute or two later, he'd put them back in.

It started to drive me crazy. It was like watching Taniqua Algernon eat her sandwich at lunch. She'd take these tiny nibbles, going slowly around the whole thing. She

51

never finished before the bell rang. It was almost as bad as waiting for Rolando Thrump to finish a sentence. He just kept getting distracted and changing the subject.

There was nothing I could do about Taniqua or Rolando, but I could at least find out what was up with Everet. At the end of study hall, I walked over, pointed to the earphones, which were on his desk, and said, "They uncomfortable?"

He shook his head. "Nope. They're the best." As he said that, he looked away, like he'd spilled some sort of secret.

"Then why do you keep taking them out?"

He shrugged. "No reason. Just a habit." He snatched the earphones up, stuffed them in his pants pocket, and walked away.

That was when I promised myself I'd get my hands on his earphones and check them out.

It wasn't easy. He kept them in his pocket. But he took his pants off for gym class. We all did, since we had to wear gym shorts.

There was no way I could sneak off the field during class. Mr. Dempsey watched us too closely for that. But there was a way I could get to Everet's locker without sneaking. We were playing touch football. He was on the other team. I waited until we were both diving for a ball. I put my head down, timing it just right, so my head rammed him in the chin.

Perfect.

My head throbbed a bit. But Everet was knocked off

his feet. His mouth hung open, and his eyes looked sort of fuzzy. As I'd hoped, the top of my head was harder than his chin.

"I'll get the nurse," I said. I dashed for the gym door before anyone could stop me. I got the nurse, just like I'd promised. But I stopped in the locker room on the way to her office.

I'd watched Everet and learned his combination. People aren't very careful about stuff like that. It was easy enough to grab the earbuds.

We had gym last period. As soon as we got out, I went behind the school and took the earbuds from my pocket. They looked pretty normal, except the tips were green instead of white. I checked to make sure they were clean. No earwax or any kind of gunk. They looked fine. The plastic felt soft and sort of warm.

I put them in, then plugged the other end into my MP3 player. Everet was right—they were comfortable. I hit the ON button.

Awesome. The music felt like it was being played live from all around me. I was bobbing in a warm ocean of sound. These earbuds were better than anything I'd ever tried. They must have cost a fortune.

I slid down against the wall of the school and sat on the grass. The music played. I wondered why Everet kept taking the earbuds out when he listened. Maybe he had sensitive ears or something.

It didn't matter. I didn't need to take them out. They felt great. I set my player on SHUFFLE, closed my eyes, and let the music swallow me. Fast songs. Slow songs. Everything sounded unbelievably good. I thought about how I'd act tomorrow if Everet reported his loss and the teachers started asking about the earbuds. It's hard to act innocent when you're guilty, but I knew I could do it. I could do a lot if it meant I got to keep these earbuds. And I was definitely keeping them. They were just too awesome to give back.

A shadow fell over me.

I opened my eyes.

Everet.

I tried to think of the best way to deal with this. I could just hand back the earbuds. What could he do? There weren't any witnesses, so there was no way he could get me in trouble for taking them. Or I could pretend they weren't his. That would be sort of cool, since I was growing really attached to them. There was no way he could prove they were his.

Yeah. That's what I'd do. Why should he have such nice ones when I enjoyed them so much? All he did with them was drive me crazy in study hall. Well, he wouldn't be doing that anymore.

"What do you want?" I asked.

"My earbuds," he said.

I could barely hear him over the music. I lowered the volume a little.

"These aren't yours," I said.

"Yes, they are. Bodztech Three-Sixty Organic Headphones."

I grinned at him. "What a coincidence. That's the same brand as mine. Bodz-whatever three something."

"Then I guess you read the warnings," he said.

"Nice try." I wasn't going to fall for any trick.

He shrugged. "Great sound. Amazing engineering. One problem." Then he smiled. It was a creepy smile. "If you leave them in your ears for more than five minutes, the buds start to grow together."

He glanced at his watch. "Wow—you've been here longer than that. A lot longer. I know. I've been watching you. I guess I'll come back and get them after they're finished. Enjoy the music while you can. It's the last thing you'll ever hear."

He turned and walked away. Idiot. Did he really think I was going to fall for— "Ouch!"

I felt a sharp pain in my head.

"Ahhgg!"

Another pain.

I reached up to yank out the earbuds.

"Aaiiieee!!!!"

The slightest pull sent a wave of agony through my head. I held the wires, clueless about what to do. The pain was steady now, like someone was slowly drilling into both my ears. I swear I could feel the buds moving toward each other, digging through my brain.

I yanked both hands as hard as I could.

The pain was unbearable.

The buds ripped free from my ears. The ends had something wet and gray smeared over them.

The pain got even worse.

The music had stopped. I couldn't hear anything. I knew I was screaming, but I couldn't even hear that.

I saw Everet strolling back toward me. I couldn't stand up. He said something. I couldn't hear the words, but I could tell what he said from the way his lips moved.

"I guess you won't be needing these anymore."

He reached out and took the earbuds from me. He unplugged my music player, dropped it in my lap, and wiped the earbuds on his shirt.

He started to walk off. Then he turned and came back. When he reached me, he leaned over and picked up my music player. Once again, I was pretty sure I knew what he was saying, even though I couldn't hear the words.

"I guess you won't need this anymore, either."

I guess not.

He walked away, leaving me alone in my pain and silence.

FOURTH AND INCHES

Go for it!" Willy screamed, nearly bouncing out of his seat and into the aisle as he stomped his feet. "Come on—get the first down!"

His team was just inches short of a first down. All they had to do was move the ball five or six inches and they'd keep possession. They were trailing by nine points with only six minutes left in the fourth quarter, so a chance to score was pretty important.

Way down below him on the field, he saw the team move into punt formation. The bad news was repeated larger than life across the stadium on the JumboTron. Willy howled in rage. Next to him, his older brother, Ken, screamed, too.

"You idiots!" he yelled.

Willy shook his head. "I don't know why we root for those guys." He winced as he watched the punt. "I knew they'd blow it."

The kick was a short one. No hang time at all. The other team ran the ball all the way back to the fifty-yard line. This was not good.

"They're total losers," Ken said.

Willy just shook his head. He couldn't believe that the team hadn't tried for a first down. How hard could it be to move the ball a couple of inches?

At least the defensive squad was half decent. They put the pressure on and managed to hold the other side at the fifty, so the team got the ball back.

But the quarterback blew two passes in a row. The first sailed out of bounds. The second got swatted down during a blitz. Then he ran, but came up short.

"Fourth and inches again. Please don't punt." Willy thought his head would pop. He knew they wouldn't go for it.

"I can't stand this!" Ken shouted. He shoved Willy on the shoulder.

Willy shoved him back. "This was your idea."

"No, it wasn't. You're the one who wanted to come." Ken shoved Willy way too hard.

"Hey!" Willy toppled out of his seat, into the aisle.

The crowd roared.

Willy looked up. He wasn't sprawled across the stadium steps. He was in the huddle. He looked down at his chest. He was wearing the quarterback's number. Ten pairs of eyes were fastened on him, waiting for his call. There was no time to think about anything. They couldn't afford a delay-of-game penalty. Not when they were just inches from a first down. It was time for action.

"Let's go for it," Willy said.

The other players all nodded.

Willy pointed to the halfback. "I'll fake a handoff. All receivers go short and cut hard. On fourteen."

The huddle broke. Willy crouched behind the center and held his hands out. He called some numbers. "Five, eleven, twenty, fourteen!"

The ball was in his hands. He spun, then faked a handoff as the halfback ran past him and dived over the blockers and defenders.

Willy looked ahead as he backpedaled. Three enormous guys had broken through the line and were charging at him like boulders rolling down a hill. He looked to his left for a receiver. He looked to his right. He looked down the field.

All he could see were helmets and shoulder pads. Everyone was moving. It looked like there were fifty or sixty players on the field. As far as Willy could tell, none of his receivers was open. For all he knew, they'd sneaked out for a hot dog.

The three big guys were almost on top of him. It seemed like a good time to change his plans.

I just need a couple inches.

Willy put his head down and tried to run to the side. The three big guys slammed into him, clamping down like bear traps.

Willy bounced off the stadium steps. He felt like he'd just spent a month in a rock tumbler.

"Those idiots!" Ken shouted, pointing to the field. "What kind of fool calls a play like that when it's fourth and inches?"

Willy crawled back into his seat and glanced at the field. The quarterback was getting up. Slowly.

"Can you believe that quarterback?" Ken asked.

"Yeah. I think I can." As everyone around him exploded in boos and hisses, Willy stood up and shouted, "Good effort! Nice try! Don't give up!"

People turned and glared at Willy, but he didn't care. They had no idea how hard it was to be the guy with the ball.

MutAnts

Die!"

Brian kicked the anthill. Then he stomped it. Then he got the hose from the side of the house and flooded it.

Soon, there was no sign of the anthill. All that remained was a puddle of mud on the bare patch of ground beneath his swing set. Brian was too old for the swing set, but he still liked to play in the backyard.

There was another anthill in the same spot the next day. Brian stomped it again.

A day later, the anthill reappeared.

"You stupid insects never learn." Brian got an old board from the basement and put it over the bare spot.

There was a hole the size of a softball in the wood the next day. A half-formed anthill jutted up through the opening. Ants swarmed around the ragged gap. Brian bent down to get a better look. Each ant carried a small piece of wood in its mouth.

He shivered as he watched. This wasn't natural. He'd seen ants carry a crumb of bread or some other spilled food. But not wood. He went to the family computer and asked a search engine, DO ANTS EAT WOOD?

The computer told him that carpenter ants ate wood. Brian looked at the picture. It was a different ant. The carpenter ant was big, black, and scary. Blown up on the computer screen, it looked like a monster. But it didn't look like the ants in his yard. They were small and brown. Brian didn't care what kind they were. He only cared about killing them.

He went to the yard and kicked the piece of wood off the bare spot. He raised his foot to stomp the hill, but then he got a better idea. He unhooked one of the metal swing seats from the rusted chains and placed it across the anthill.

"Eat this," he said as he stomped down on the seat. Little bits of wood and sawdust flew out from under the seat. Brian stomped again and again, until the anthill was flattened, the seat was jammed into the ground, and he was panting and sweating.

He stayed out of the backyard for a week.

When he finally went to check, the seat was gone. So was one whole leg of the swing set. Ants swarmed over the three remaining legs. The anthill was back, taller than ever.

"No! Die!" Brian kicked the anthill. Then he stamped

on the nearest mass of ants. He raised his foot, hoping to see a smeared mess of dead insects.

Instead, he saw living ants.

He stomped again. He screamed. He kept stomping until his sneaker fell apart.

"What?"

Brian raised his leg and stared at the laced-together pieces that dangled from his foot. The sneaker was shredded. As the sun moved out from behind a cloud, a flash of light caught Brian's attention. He bent over.

The ants shone like steel, reflecting the sun.

As he stood there, they swarmed up his legs.

Brian brushed at them. Their sharp edges cut his fingers. They clung to his pants. He brushed harder. More ants swarmed.

Brian turned to run. He couldn't. The weight of the metal ants pulled him to the ground.

He fell, screaming, as hundreds more ants swarmed over him.

The screams didn't last long.

The sun moved back behind a cloud. Right before it disappeared, some of the ants flashed and glistened. Others seemed to grow duller, colored almost like flesh. The metallic ants returned to the remains of the swing set, hungry for more metal. The flesh ants milled toward the rear door of the house. They were hungry, too.

CAT GOT YOUR NOSE?

"Can I have a cat?" Emily asked.

"No, sweetie," her mom said. "I'm sorry."

"No way," her dad said. "Cats stink."

Most kids would have worked on Mom, since she was the softer of the two parents. But Emily was stunningly clever, and knew it was much easier to hit a target you could see. Mom hadn't given any real objection. Dad had lobbed a softball right over the plate.

"Cats don't stink," Emily said.

"Sure they do," Dad said. "You know what it's like at Miss Reaker's house."

Miss Reaker lived on the next block. She loved animals, and was always happy to take in stray cats. And though Miss Reaker's house did smell a bit catty, this was exactly the answer Emily was hoping for, because it allowed her to keep her argument going.

"That doesn't count. Miss Reaker has fifteen cats. I just want one. It won't stink."

"It will stink less," Dad said. "But it will still stink. A big stink divided by fifteen is still a stink."

Emily opened her mouth. Her dad held up his hand. "Cats stink. End of discussion."

End of discussion, perhaps, but the beginning of Emily's quest. She went to the library to read every book and magazine article she could find about smells, odors, aromas, and scents. It took her five months to learn what she needed, and another two months to perfect her anti-stink formula.

During that whole agonizing time, she never even uttered the word *cat* in the presence of either of her parents. But now the time had come.

"Dad, if cats didn't stink, could I have one?" she asked after she'd put the final version of the formula into a small squirt bottle.

He laughed. "Sure."

"Promise?"

"Absolutely. I think it's a safe promise, because cats stink. And there's nothing you can do about it."

"Can we go visit Miss Reaker?" Emily asked.

Dad wrinkled his nose, but then said, "Okay. But just a quick visit."

Emily liked visiting Miss Reaker. She made wonderful cookies, as long as you didn't mind a bit of cat hair among the chocolate chips, and the occasional little crunchy thing that was better left unidentified.

When they reached Miss Reaker's house, she greeted them with a cat clutched in each of her arms. "Come in. It's been so long since I've had visitors. I'll go make tea." She scurried off toward the kitchen. A half-dozen cats raced after her, meowing, and three more strays slipped inside through the open door.

Emily and her dad went in. Emily had to admit that the place did stink more than a little bit. She could see her dad wrinkling his nose. But not for long. She whipped the spray bottle from her pocket and gave it a squeeze, squirting the formula on a passing Siamese cat. She scooped up the cat and thrust it under her dad's nose.

"Hey, stop that!" he shouted as he backed away.

"Smell anything?" Emily asked Dad after she put the cat back down.

He sniffed the air. Then he sniffed again. Then he drew in a gigantic breath through his nose. "This is amazing. I don't smell those stinky cats. How'd you do it?"

"Doesn't matter," Emily said. "Can we go to the rescue shelter after we leave here? I'd like to get my cat today."

"Look, there's no way—"

"You promised," Emily said. She fought to keep the smile of triumph from spreading across her lips. There was nothing to be gained by gloating. But she'd won, and she knew it. Dad might be strict at times, but he was always fair.

"I guess I did promise," Dad said. "And I'll keep my word. You'll get a cat. Maybe you can have one of Miss Reaker's cats."

Miss Reaker, who'd returned from the kitchen with three cups of weak tea and a stacked plate of cookies, nodded. "Take a cat. Take two. I can get lots more. They show up all the time."

"Thank you," Emily said. "That's a wonderful offer. But I want my very own kitten." She could already see herself cuddling her new pet.

After they finished their visit with Miss Reaker, they headed for the shelter. Emily hoped the shelter would have a tangerine-colored long-furred little girl kitten with green eyes. And she hoped the kitten would purr in her arms and fall asleep. But more than anything else, she hoped her dad would let her adopt the kitten before he realized he couldn't smell anything at all. That's how her formula worked.

His sense of smell would come back in a while, but by then, Emily was sure he'd love her kitten just as much as she did.

THE RIDE OF A LIFETIME

I've been waiting all my life for this," Zack said as he got his first glimpse of the Titanium Tempest from the entrance to the parking lot.

The steel rails of the world's fastest, highest, and newest roller coaster burst from the center of the park, twisting and looping like a robot's intestines. Zack was still too far away to hear the clack of the wheels as the cars hurtled around the track or the screams that marked the wildest scares on the mile-long high-speed panic ride, but he could imagine the sounds, and he could imagine what his own shrieks of joy would be like when he plunged down that first awesome eighty-degree drop.

Ever since he'd been tall enough to ride the real coasters, Zack had been a coaster fanatic. If it was possible, he'd ride all day. When he'd heard about the Titanium Tempest, he'd begged his parents to go to Wild Action Park for vacation.

And here they were.

The best part was that they'd arrived early in the day. Better yet—it was the middle of the week, and there'd been just a little bit of rain right after sunrise. The crowds weren't heavy. Zack figured that even if everyone in the park headed for the Titanium Tempest, the lines wouldn't be too bad right now. Later in the afternoon, when the park filled to capacity, the wait would grow unbearable.

"Totally awesome," Zack said. He started to list the statistics he'd memorized about the coaster: "Five thousand three hundred feet of track. Nine loops."

"Get a life," his big sister, Tara, said. "It's just a stupid ride. It doesn't even last that long. Whoosh—it's over. Why bother?"

"You get a life," Zack told her. He knew what Tara would do. She'd spend the whole day in the park staring at boys. Or, more accurately, trying to get boys to look at her. Zack didn't care about stuff like that. He planned to get in line and ride the Tempest as many times as he could. Front car. Back car. Middle cars. He'd try them all.

"What do you kids want to do first?" his dad asked as he pulled into a parking space.

"The pool," Tara said.

"That sounds nice," Zack's mom said.

Zack groaned. There were pools everywhere. The planet was covered with swimming pools. Half their neighbors had pools. So what if this one was bigger and had a wave machine. Who cared?

"Rides," Zack said. "That's what we came for."

"That's what you came for," Tara said.

"The pool sounds perfect," Zack's dad said. "We've got all day. No point in rushing around. We're on vacation, after all. We came here to relax."

"Well, can I go by myself?" Zack asked. He'd come here to get flung in five directions at once.

"Absolutely not," his mom said.

Zack argued all the way to the pool, only giving up when his mother issued a warning for him to stop whining, backed by a harsh stare from his dad.

Stupid pool.

Zack sat on the artificial beach and glared at the artificial waves. He wasn't going to give his parents the satisfaction of seeing him play in the water. What a way to waste the morning. Worst of all, the third curve of the Tempest, complete with a double corkscrew, jutted over one side of the pool. Zack was so close, he could see the thrilled faces of the riders as they flashed past.

Finally, his dad stretched, looked around, and said, "Well, I don't know about the rest of you, but I'm ready for something more exciting."

"About time," Zack muttered. He shivered as a small cloud passed in front of the sun. The day was barely warm enough for swimming.

His mom nodded. "Lunch would be nice."

"Lunch?" Zack gasped. He knew what that meant— another wasted hour as they wandered from restaurant to restaurant, staring at the menus in the windows, trying to find a place that would satisfy everyone. Zack was sure that no such place existed anywhere on the planet. His mom liked fancy food, his dad liked simple stuff, and his sister would only eat food that had no fat, no sugar, no preservatives, and as far as Zack could tell, no flavor. He couldn't remember the last time the family had ordered a pepperoni pizza.

Eventually, they settled on a sandwich shop—a compromise nob ly seemed to want but everyone seemed willing to tolerate.

By the end of lunch, there was one monster of a line snaking around the base of the Titanium Tempest. "Can I ride that coaster?" Zack asked. "Please?"

"The line's kind of long," his mother said.

"I know it's long!" Zack shouted. "That's because we spent all morning in the stupid pool!"

"Zack," his dad said, "watch your mouth, or you'll be spending all afternoon in the motel."

Zack opened his mouth, but he managed to keep from shouting the angry words that bounced around inside his skull. *Please,* he thought, willing his dad to give him permission. *That's all I want. Please. Please. Please.*

"Oh, get in the stupid line," his dad said. "Meet us at the bumper cars when you're done."

"*Yes!*" Zack ran to the line before his mom could overrule his dad. As the endless trail of humanity inched forward, he tried to decide where he wanted to sit for his very first ride. There was always a longer wait for the front car. He'd save that for later. Right now, he'd take whatever he could get.

An hour passed, and finally Zack was in the last stretch. He moved up the steps that led to the loading area. Just ahead, beyond the turnstile, the riders flowed into one of fourteen chutes that led to the fourteen pairs of seats on the Titanium Tempest.

"Soon," Zack whispered.

He squeezed through the turnstile and looked ahead. Most of the lines were about the same, but Zack was a pro. He picked the line with the most couples. Lines with single riders—riders like Zack—would take longer. People usually didn't want to ride with a stranger on a coaster.

Zack moved closer. There were only three couples ahead of him. Then two. He watched people as they stumbled off the ride. They all looked like they'd been shaken nearly to pieces and whacked hard on the head at least a half-dozen times. Perfect. That was the kind of ride he loved.

Finally, the last pair between him and hapiness boarded the Tempest. Zack had made it to the front of the line. The car moved out and crawled up the long climb. As it reached the crest and hurtled down the drop, another rumble mixed with the roar of the coaster.

Thunder.

Please no, Zack thought.

There was a second rumble. Then, as the car returned from the ride, a flash and a crack.

The sky drowned Zack's hopes with buckets of rain.

"We're sorry, the Tempest is closed until further notice," the operator said over the loudspeaker.

"No!" Zack watched in envy and agony as the last riders climbed out of the cars. *I hate them,* he thought.

Zack walked to the bumper cars, not caring if he got drenched. All around him, people clustered under anything that offered shelter. At least nobody else was having fun.

He found his parents. Together, they waited for the rain to stop. It finally did, but lightning kept flashing for the rest of the afternoon, keeping the Titanium Tempest closed.

Zack rode other rides, but each mild spin on a Scrambler or a Ferris wheel just made him more and more miserable. Toward evening, the clouds thinned, then faded. But by the time the Titanium Tempest opened again and Zack got permission to go back, the line was three times as long as before. Zack could do the math. It was nine o'clock. The park closed at eleven. The people at the end of the line would never reach the ride.

"Stupid losers," he muttered. Zack cursed and turned away from the Titanium Tempest. He didn't even want to look at it now. Not if he couldn't ride it. As he walked away, to meet back up with his parents, he bumped into a little kid.

"Watch it!" Zack lashed out and shoved the kid, hoping he could knock him off his feet.

The kid stumbled away without looking back. A flutter of white caught Zack's eye. Something had fallen from the kid's hand. Zack stooped and reached down.

"Hey!" he called after the kid. "Wait."

Then he read what he held. ADMIT ONE, the ticket promised. Below that were words Zack almost couldn't believe. TAKE A MIDNIGHT RIDE ON THE TITANIUM TEMPEST.

As the kid turned back, Zack dodged into the crowd. No way he was giving this up. A midnight ride. That had to be special. And if he had a ticket, he'd absolutely get his ride.

Now he just had to figure out how to slip away from his parents. As he thought about other family trips they'd taken, he realized it wouldn't be hard to escape. His parents rarely stayed up late. And his sister never paid any attention to what he was doing.

When the family was sitting around the motel room after dinner, Zack could see his mom and dad were getting sleepy. He pulled out the convertible couch and sprawled across the mattress, but he kept his clothes on. By eleven thirty, he could hear his dad snoring in the bedroom. Across the room, his sister sat on the other couch, watching television. Zack got up and walked to the door. As he turned the knob, he glanced back at his sister. She didn't look away from the television.

"Going for a walk," he muttered.

Ahead, the park was nearly dark. But the Titanium Tempest, flashing all thirty thousand of its lights, called him like a beacon. Zack felt in his pocket for the ticket and wondered if it was good for just one ride. Free pass. That's what it had said.

He reached the entrance to the park. Nobody was there.

But the gate was open. Zack wove his way through the paths leading up to the Titanium Tempest, then climbed the steps.

"Hello?" he called out. Maybe it was a mistake. Maybe he had the wrong day. He pulled out the ticket and checked it. No date. Just midnight. A wooden sign standing next to the turnstile read: NO ADMISSION WITHOUT A TICKET.

"No problem," Zack said.

He pushed through the turnstile.

"Anybody here?" he called.

Silence.

But the empty cars were there, waiting on the track.

Zack walked up to the front car and sat down, taking the seat on the left. He'd already figured, based on the layout of the track, that the left side would be the wildest.

He heard a hiss as the safety bar came down. Then he felt a jolt as the car lurched forward.

"Cool," Zack said, barely able to believe his luck. He was going to get a ride. In the front car. All by himself.

The car climbed at a steep angle, pressing him against the seat. *Here it comes,* Zack thought as the car leveled out. For a smooth second, he moved straight ahead. Then the world dropped out from under him and he plummeted toward the earth.

Awesome.

A sharp turn jolted the car to the right.

"Ow!" Zack shouted as his left shoulder banged against the side of the car. The ticket flew from his hand. He realized it didn't matter. He was already on the ride. Nothing could stop him now.

The car snaked to the left, then shot back to the right, slamming Zack again. He reached the first loop and braced himself against the force of acceleration.

When the car shot out of the loop, Zack was jolted twice to the right, banging his left shoulder again. Then a sharp jerk from another turn slammed his knees against the front of the car, sending a burst of pain through his legs.

As the ride reached the last drop and curve, Zack relaxed his clenched grip. He'd never been shaken this hard on a steel coaster. It must have been the empty cars, he realized. That was why the ride was so rough. The Titanium Tempest was designed to run best when full.

At least it's over, he thought as the car approached the loading platform. He got ready to climb out.

"Wait," Zack gasped as the car sped past the platform and headed back up the hill.

He yanked at the safety bar.

It was locked solidly around him. He looked over his shoulder. The back side of the sign by the turnstile had a message, too. NO EXIT WITHOUT A TICKET.

No exit? Zack yanked harder at the safety bar as the car climbed the steep hill, but the bar didn't move.

The second ride was just as rough as the first. The third might have been even rougher.

Zack tried to hold himself still. He struggled to keep from being slammed and bruised, but his strength gave out. Eventually, battered, banged, and slammed, he let go and flopped inside the car, waiting for day. Waiting for light that never came. Waiting for the endless ride to end.

CHIRP

*S*ean Unquist had the strangest problem: Whenever he said, "Chirp," he turned into a bird. He didn't stay a bird for more than a moment, and he didn't always turn into the same kind of bird, but he always turned into some kind of bird.

As inconvenient as this was, Sean realized he was lucky. He rarely said *chirp* by accident. If the word that changed him had been *hello, feather,* or some other common word, Sean knew he'd have been in a lot more trouble.

He'd been by himself the first time it happened, and had kept this secret to himself forever. His parents didn't know. His brothers and sisters didn't know. His best friend didn't know. But the secret needed to be shared. And when Jennifer Marie Starkholder moved in right across the street from him, Sean knew he'd found the perfect person to share his secret. Jennifer looked—well, she just looked so understanding.

And she obviously loved birds. She owned seven different shirts with pictures of birds—Sean had counted—along with a lunch box decorated with cardinals, earrings in the shape of hummingbirds, and a variety of bird drawings on her book covers.

The very first time Sean met her, as soon as he saw the lunch box, the earrings, and the first of those seven shirts, he almost blurted out his secret. But he'd waited. He wanted to tell her, but he was afraid she'd laugh at him and walk away. He couldn't imagine anything worse than that.

Finally, a month after she arrived, he spotted her filling the bird feeder by her living room window. He crossed the street, went up to her, and said, "I turn into a bird." He held his breath and watched her expression, hoping she wouldn't laugh in his face.

Jennifer didn't laugh. She didn't tell him he was imagining things. She didn't mock him or sneer. Instead, she said, "How does it happen?"

"I just say . . ." Sean paused. He didn't want to become a bird in front of the house, where anyone might see.

"Let's go into my backyard," Jennifer said.

Sean followed her around the side of the house. It was a nice yard, with a small birdbath and two more bird feeders. Like his own yard, it was surrounded with bushes. Strangers wouldn't see him become a bird. Sean checked to make sure Jennifer was watching him. He was pleased that he had her full attention.

"Chirp," he said.

He became a sparrow and stayed that way for about a minute. That's how long the change usually lasted.

"See," Sean said when he became a boy again.

"I see," Jennifer said. "I love birds so much. Did you know that sparrows give themselves dust baths? But they aren't afraid of water. People have actually seen them swim underwater. Isn't that amazing?"

"Yeah, it sure is," Sean said.

"Do it again. It would be wonderful to see something rare."

Sean did it again. He became a stork.

"Again, please," Jennifer said.

Sean became a robin, and then a crow, and then a goldfinch. Jennifer told him fascinating facts about each bird and asked him to keep going.

"There are birds I've heard about but never seen," she said.

"I don't know if this is such a good idea," Sean told her. "I might become a hawk and attack you. Some birds have razor-sharp claws." He flinched at the idea of scratching her.

Jennifer shook her head. "I feel safe with you. I'm sure you'd never hurt me. Keep changing."

Sean kept changing.

"There we go," Jennifer said after one of the changes. "Finally."

Sean couldn't answer. He couldn't talk when he was a bird.

"An auk," Jennifer said. "Just what I was waiting for. A

nice plump bird that can't fly. No dangerous claws. No sharp beak. How lovely," she said, clapping her hands together and smiling. "But, Sean, you aren't as special as you think. I have a word that changes me, too."

Jennifer knelt on the lawn and grinned at Sean. The grin became a laugh. Then she opened her mouth and said, "Meow."

"Awk!" Sean screeched as the cat pounced.

Jennifer Marie Starkholder had a secret. And a meal.

BRUJA

Stella is the meanest sister in the world. She got even meaner after I killed her neon tetras last month. All five of them. It wasn't my fault. I didn't want to feed her fish while she was at camp, but she told me I had to. She knows I have a hard time remembering stuff. Mom is always nagging me to pick up my clothes, and Dad has to remind me to do my chores.

Maybe I should have put the can of fish food in my room where I'd see it. I didn't know they'd die that quickly. I didn't even know they were dead until I heard the scream from her room the day she got back.

"You let them die!" She stormed down the stairs and chased after me.

Mom saved me. But Stella has been glaring at me ever since then. I know she's thinking up some terrible way to get even. And I know it won't happen for a while. I've seen Stella in action. When someone gets her angry, she thinks and plots and waits until the perfect moment. And then she does terrible things.

It was bad enough when we were at home. At least I knew how to keep out of her way. But we're on vacation this week. Dad took us all to Mexico—me, Stella, Mom, and my little brother, Kaleb.

It's not as much fun as it sounds. Everything is hot and sticky and strange. We'd spent a couple days in Mexico City, but now we're in this small town with a name I can't pronounce. The name has three *x*'s in it, and five letters in a row without a vowel. Mom and Dad were going to take a tour of some caves to see these stupid old paintings. I didn't want to go, but I didn't want to stay in the room with Stella.

"Can I go to the *mercado?*" I asked. That's what they call a store here. There was a shop right down the block from the hotel.

Mom looked at Dad. Dad looked at Mom. They both looked at me. "I'll be careful," I said.

"It's safe here," Dad said to Mom.

Mom nodded.

"Okay," Dad said.

"Thanks." I headed out for the shop. There wasn't much to see, but there was no way I was going back into the room with Stella. Not when my parents weren't around to keep her from getting her revenge.

Then, when I was in the far corner of the shop, looking

at these really scary masks, I saw her come in through the front door. She hadn't spotted me yet. I slipped out a side door.

Where to go?

I walked down the street, away from the hotel. Half a block later, a little boy ran up to me. I got ready to tell him I didn't have any money. That wasn't true. Mom always made me carry a couple dollars. Or pesos, I guess. But there were lots of beggar kids in the city, so I expected this kid to be like them.

Instead, he said, "You are worried."

"What?"

"Worried. Yes?"

He had an accent, but I could understand him.

I nodded, unsure how safe it was to talk with a stranger—even if he was half my size.

"The *bruja*—she can help you."

"*Bruja?*"

He nodded and pointed down the street. "Come—it isn't far. I'll show you."

I looked over my shoulder to make sure Stella hadn't left the *mercado*, then followed him. Two blocks later, he stopped in front of a tiny shop. The building was barely wider than the door.

"In there," he said.

"You go first."

He nodded and opened the door. I took a step away from the hot street. The air was definitely cooler inside.

An old woman was sitting at a table. There was a second chair on the other side.

The woman said something in Spanish.

"Come," the boy said. "Tell her your troubles."

As I spoke, the boy translated my words into Spanish. "My sister hates me. She asked me to feed her fish. I forgot. They died." I paused after each sentence so he could keep up with me. When I was done, the woman glanced at a row of shelves on the wall behind her, then spoke again.

"There is a way to help," the boy said.

The woman got up from the table and walked to the shelves. She took down three bottles, poured a couple drops from each into a smaller bottle, then placed that bottle on the table. Each of the three liquids was clear, but the mixture turned black. A smell like licorice and woodsmoke filled the air.

Again, the boy translated when the woman spoke.

"Pour this over the grave of the fish. They will come back to life. Dig them up immediately and put them in water. Your sister will forgive you."

I stared at the bottle. It didn't seem possible. But maybe that didn't matter. Even if I couldn't bring the dead fish back to life, this would show Stella that I'd tried. And then maybe she'd forgive me.

I felt the crumpled bills in my pants pocket. "How much?"

The woman answered before the boy could translate my words. I guess she knew what I was asking.

"That is up to you," the boy said.

I put several twenty-peso notes on the table and picked up the bottle. *"Gracias."* That was about the only word I knew in Spanish, besides *mercado.*

"Vaya con Dios," the woman said.

I stepped into the brutal light of the outside world and found myself face-to-face with Stella.

"What are you doing?" she asked. "I've been looking all over for you."

"Nothing." I put my hand behind my back. I wanted to surprise her when we got home. We could try to save the fish together. If I told her now, she'd probably just stay angry.

"What do you have? Give it to me." She thrust her hand out.

I turned and ran.

She chased after me.

I was a good runner. I didn't escape, but I managed to stay far enough ahead of her that she couldn't grab me. People stared at us, but nobody did anything to help me. I guess they could tell it was a family thing. I saw a church straight ahead. I ran up the steps and flung open the door. Someone in there would help me.

It was empty. My footsteps echoed on the floor. I raced down the aisle between the bare wood pews.

"I'm gonna get you," Stella screamed. "You are so dead!"

That gave me another burst of speed. I saw a doorway with stairs to my left. I turned and raced down. The air felt even cooler than in the *bruja's* shop. There was a tunnel ahead, past a brick archway.

Bad idea? Was I trapped? It was too late to worry. I ran ahead. The tunnel turned and twisted. Light flickered. I realized the walls were lined with torches.

I went deeper. This couldn't be just a basement. It seemed to stretch on for a long way. I wasn't even sure we were still under the church.

Someone grabbed my shoulder. I screamed.

Stella. She'd caught me. She spun me around, grabbed my wrist, and stared at my hand.

"You're too young for perfume." She pried the bottle from my fingers.

I opened my mouth to tell her it wasn't perfume. Then I opened my mouth even wider. I finally took a good look around. The walls—all of them—were made of bones. Arm bones. Leg bones. Skulls. Thousands of bones. Maybe hundreds of thousands.

I pointed. But Stella was so angry, she couldn't see anything but me. "Whatever you buy—I'll destroy it. Whatever you want, I'll take it away. Whatever you care about—I'll ruin it. I'm going to make you miserable for the rest of your life. Starting right now."

She turned and flung the bottle against the wall of bones.

The glass shattered. Liquid splashed over the skeletons. I guess that's when Stella finally noticed where we were.

She screamed.

The bones moved.

The whole wall rattled like an earthquake had struck. The bones shook like chattering teeth. One by one at first, and then in clusters, they fell from the wall and hit the floor.

But they didn't scatter.

They pulled together.

One of the skeletons stood. It turned toward us. Others joined us. The whole wall collapsed. More skeletons rose from the pile. They blocked the way out.

Stella screamed again. So did I.

"Stupid fish," I whispered as the skeletons surged toward us, swinging their arms like clubs and snapping their jaws.

I knew I'd never get out of there. Stella was right. I'd be miserable for the rest of my life. That was true for sure, because my life wouldn't last much longer. But at least I didn't have to wonder what Stella would do to punish me for this, because she wasn't getting out of here, either.

ELF IMPROVEMENT

The first time he saw the elf, Gerald was at his desk in the next-to-last row of Ms. Crukshank's fifth-grade classroom, wrestling with the final problem on a math worksheet and enjoying the breeze drifting in through the open window to his left.

As he was double-checking his answer, a motion caught his attention. Gerald was too stunned to do more than make a quiet gurgling sound when the elf scrambled up the side of his desk.

Actually, he wasn't even sure whether the creature was an elf or some other tiny troublemaker like a pixie or a sprite. But that didn't matter. The only thing that mattered was that Gerald's life suddenly became a lot less fun and a lot more stressful.

The elf, who was dressed in brown pants and a plain white shirt, picked up Gerald's pencil box and threw it out the window. Then he reached up, lifted his green cap from his head, grinned at Gerald, and bowed.

As his plastic case full of pencils and markers went plummeting two stories down toward the pavement, Gerald managed to blurt out, "Hey!" and point at the elf. "Look!"

At that same instant, the elf leaped off the desk and disappeared behind a bookcase underneath the window. Also at that same instant, Ms. Crukshank turned toward Gerald.

Gerald's shout died. But it was followed a split second later by the smack of his pencil box smashing to the ground.

"Gerald," Ms. Crukshank said, "I will not tolerate this kind of stunt in my classroom. You know we have rules about the window."

"But I . . ." Gerald had no idea how to defend himself. The last time he'd shouted, when Tommy Pratt swiped his eraser, he had to stay after school. And Tommy hadn't gotten in any trouble at all. Life wasn't fair.

For the rest of the day, Gerald kept expecting the elf to return. It didn't. But Gerald was so stressed, he felt like he was trying to crush a giant aluminum can inside his stomach.

The elf showed up the next day, just in time to knock over the jar of poster paint Gerald was using for his geography project. Ms. Crukshank not only made him clean up the mess, she also made him stay after school and write a three-page paper about carelessness and wasting valuable classroom supplies.

Gerald thought about telling her the truth, but every time he imagined himself trying to explain about the elf, he also imagined his teacher shouting at him and making him write a five-page report on the dangers of having an overactive imagination.

The next day, the elf broke the tips off of all Gerald's pencils. He had to sharpen them several times. Finally, Ms. Crukshank told him he couldn't use the sharpener anymore.

The day after that, the elf ripped up Gerald's homework. Gerald had to stay inside at recess and do it over.

Life really wasn't fair.

The next day, Gerald tried to catch the elf. He waited and waited, ready to grab it the moment it showed up.

It didn't show up. But Gerald got in trouble for not paying attention in class. Ms. Crukshank told him he had to stay after and clean the blackboards.

As the rest of the kids were leaving the room, Gerald saw the elf climbing up the leg of his desk. He lunged for it.

The elf leaped from the desk. Gerald's fingers swiped across its back, snagging its shirt. When he tried to make another grab, Gerald slipped off his chair and fell to the floor. The elf got away.

"Gerald!" Ms. Crukshank shouted, "get off the floor this instant."

Gerald sprang to his feet with the elf's shirt in his hand. He had proof! Finally.

He ran over to his teacher's desk. "Look, Ms. Crukshank! See?" He thrust his palm under her nose.

"Ick!" Ms. Crukshank shouted. "Don't shove your dirty tissues in my face, you grubby boy." She grabbed the giant pump bottle of hand sanitizer she always kept on her desk and blasted Gerald's hand with a double shot. It knocked the shirt right out of his hand and onto the floor.

Ms. Crukshank snatched a couple tissues from the box on her desk, scooped up the soggy shirt, and tossed everything in the garbage. "Filthy boys," she muttered as she left the room. "You're all just walking sacks full of germs."

"But . . ." Gerald watched her go. Then he sighed and started cleaning the chalkboards.

Life really really wasn't fair.

As Gerald was leaving school after cleaning the blackboards, he passed the cafeteria, where the teachers were having a meeting. He glanced in the door as he went by.

Ms. Crukshank was sitting right next to the principal, Ms. Owens. Gerald almost kept going, but something caught his eye. A shirtless elf was climbing up the table leg next to Ms. Crukshank. Even from this distance, Gerald could tell the elf was grinning.

It got up to the top of the table, then kicked over Ms. Crukshank's coffee cup just as she was reaching for it.

"Yipe!" Principal Owens screeched as hot coffee poured into her lap.

Gerald watched as Ms. Crukshank apologized and fussed and looked all flustered. Then he smiled and walked out of the school. Maybe life wasn't fair, but at least it wasn't fair all around.

That, Gerald decided, almost made things fair.

SUN DAMAGE

He was chained to the wall in a room hidden beneath a trapdoor in the basement. "I call him Fang," Roy told me. He shined the flashlight beam at the man.

I'd always thought *gooseflesh* was just an expression, but I could feel my arms twitching like my skin wanted to escape from the room. "This is too creepy."

The room was just a hole, really, dug into the floor of the basement. Maybe six feet wide, with cinder block walls and a dirt floor. Nothing in it except for a ladder against the wall beneath the opening, and a pair of iron rings attached to the opposite wall. And the guy, of course.

"Sort of cool, though," Roy said.

I kept my back pressed against the wall next to the ladder. I didn't want to get too close to the guy. If he'd been down here for a while—and he had to have been, since nobody had lived in this house for years—he was far from human. Kids had been sneaking into the house for ages, but I'm pretty sure Roy was the first one to discover the room.

"What's he doing here?" I asked.

"I don't know. I guess someone wanted to keep him locked up. Maybe he's dangerous." Roy bent down. "Watch this."

He picked up a jagged piece of stone from the floor. Before I could say anything, he jabbed the guy in the arm, slicing his skin open.

I shouted. The guy didn't. As my cry died against the barren walls, the shallow wound pulled together and the flesh healed itself.

"I think he's a vampire," Roy said.

The guy flinched. It was slight, barely more than a shiver. But there was no doubt he'd reacted to Roy's words.

"You're right." I'd always been good at reading people. I took a step closer. But I stayed a safe distance away. "You're a vampire, aren't you?"

His lips moved. I watched his face, looking for a reaction that would prove I was right. He spoke, but it was too quiet for me to hear. I took another step. Then I froze. "You won't trick me that easily." He'd tried to lure me close enough to hurt me. Nice try. But I wasn't stupid.

I backed away. His head drooped. I almost felt sorry for him, trapped here for who knew how long, living in total darkness.

As if he could read my mind, he said, "Some of us are harmed by sunlight."

"That would be totally cool," Roy said. "Crackle, crackle, whoosh. Just like in the movies. We could drag him out into the sun."

I shook my head. "No way. We're not touching those chains."

To my relief, Roy nodded. "Yeah, you're right." He lowered the flashlight. I heard Fang sigh as the darkness fell across his face again. I guess he didn't even like artificial light.

"Let's get out of here." I put my foot on the first rung of the ladder that was against the wall opposite Fang.

Before I could climb up, Roy shouted, "I got it!"

"What?"

He turned the flashlight back toward Fang. "We can bring the sunlight here."

"How?"

"Mirrors."

This time, the guy did more than quiver. He jerked his hands against the chains and screamed, "No!"

I watched the wall. The rings holding the chains were solid. Fang had no chance of breaking free.

"Oh, we definitely gotta do this now," Roy said.

"Definitely." I liked the way Fang squirmed at the idea. I wondered how much more he'd thrash around when we actually brought down the sunlight. "Hey, let's make a video!"

"Awesome." Roy held his hands up like he was pointing a camera at Fang. "We'll post it online and get a zillion hits."

It took us a couple days to find enough mirrors. I borrowed two from my house, and Roy had one in his attic. I don't know where he got the others.

We had to wait a couple more days, until the rainy weather passed. But on a brilliant Saturday morning, with no clouds at all in the sky, we started setting up the mirrors.

"Kind of like a video game," Roy said as he placed the first mirror in the front yard. The reflected light hit the door.

"Yeah, except we already know how to beat the boss at the end of the level." I opened the front door and put the next mirror in the hall, sending the light past the door to the basement. Roy got everything on video, but he made sure not to show our faces. We didn't want to get in trouble like those idiots who film their fistfights or vandalism sprees.

It was harder than we expected to get the light all the way to the basement. Especially getting the beam down the stairs. We had to prop that mirror at an angle. But finally, we reached the trapdoor above the pit. One more mirror, placed down in the floor of the hidden room, and Fang would be hit right in the face by a beam of sunlight.

He looked up at us through the opening. I studied his eyes for any sign of terror, but he just seemed tired.

"Don't," he said. "You'll regret it."

I almost felt sorry for him. Almost. I grabbed the last

mirror. "Nothing personal," I said. "We just can't miss our chance. Something this awesome probably only comes around once in a lifetime." I'd fried ants with a magnifying glass when I was little. And Roy and I burned a wasps' nest once. But this would be way more exciting.

"Hold on." Roy took off his shirt and draped it over the next-to-last mirror. "I want to see this from close up." He found a piece of rope in the basement and tied it to the shirt.

Roy and I climbed down into the pit. Then I placed the last mirror where the beam would strike the floor, and aimed it at Fang's face.

"Ready?" Roy asked.

"Totally." I hoped I'd placed the last mirror right.

"Time to sizzle!" Roy pulled the rope. The shirt slipped down. Light bounced off the last mirror, striking Fang right in the face. I'd placed everything perfectly.

Fang's body jerked. He arched his back and howled like he was being jolted with a billion volts of electricity.

I watched, waiting for smoke to rise from his flesh. The little bit of remaining guilt was replaced by excitement. I was going to see something legendary. How many kids could say that?

There was still no smoke. It was a moment before I realized Fang's skin was changing in a different way.

"He's getting younger!" I shouted. "Knock over the mirror!"

Roy kicked at the mirror on the floor.

Fang thrust his hands forward. Both chains snapped.

He sprang straight off the wall with a leap that took him to the other side of the pit.

He grabbed Roy by the hair and threw him down hard against the floor, right by my feet. He stood there, bathed in light from the mirror above us.

"Some creatures are harmed by the sun." Fang stepped toward me.

I flattened myself against the wall. Roy was twitching like he'd been hurt pretty badly.

Fang moved closer. "But some creatures gain strength from the sun. I'm not one of those pale-faced blood-drinkers. I prefer my meals to be a bit more solid."

He held up one hand with his fingers rigid. Light flashed off the tips. "Perhaps *Claws* would have been a better nickname for me."

He thrust his hand down, spearing it right into Roy's back, and pulled something out. Roy screamed once, then stopped moving.

I pressed harder against the wall. "Don't hurt me."

"Nothing personal. I just can't miss my chance." Fang thrust his hand toward me. As pain exploded through my body, I heard him say, "It's so nice to be back."

SWEET SOAP

Barnaby Pointdexter, the world's youngest inventor, stood before his greatest invention, ready to run the first test. Built from an assortment of old parts he'd found in the basement and a few new pieces he'd bought with his allowance, the Transubstantiator would change the world. Barnaby was sure of that.

"How's it work?" his sister, Myra, asked.

"Very complicated," Barnaby said. "Hard to explain."

"In other words," Myra said, "you really don't know."

Barnaby shrugged. "I guess you could say that. But it doesn't matter whether I know how it works. As long as it works, I'm happy. Now, hand me that soap."

"Yes, Your Majesty," Myra said, her voice hinting that she wouldn't take too many orders from her brother.

"Thanks." Barnaby put the bar of soap into the container in the middle of the Transubstantiator. The soap was an extra-large bar that Barnaby had snatched from his parents' bathroom cabinet. The container was an old butter tub. There was no longer any butter in it.

"Ready?" Barnaby asked.

"I guess."

"Here goes." Barnaby put his finger on the button, then froze. He realized that *here goes* was a pretty unimpressive statement. He really needed to make a great and memorable quotation on this special occasion. He took a deep breath, then said, "I do this for all my fellow humans." Then he pressed the button.

The Transubstantiator sprang into action, chugging and huffing and making a wide assortment of sounds normally associated with an automobile that is about to stop running or explode. When all the grinding and buzzing faded back into silence, and the last moving parts became motionless, Barnaby reached inside the container and removed the soap.

"Well?" Myra asked.

Barnaby sniffed the soap. "I think it isn't soap anymore. I think it's candy." He took a bite.

"Well?" Myra asked again. She wasn't alarmed. She'd seen her brother put things far more dreadful than soap in his mouth.

For a moment, Barnaby was so excited, he couldn't speak. This was fabulous. He'd succeeded beyond his wildest dreams.

"Here, try it."

Myra, less eager than Barnaby, took a sniff. "It does smell sort of good." Then she took a small bite. An instant later, she took a large chomp. "This is great!" she said between mouthfuls.

"Sure is. It tastes like all my favorite candies mixed together." Barnaby ran through the house, collecting more soap. After he and Myra had eaten their fill, he started sharing his invention with the world. Soon, every home had a Transubstantiator.

Around the world, people were turning soap into candy. It was fabulous. It was delicious. It was great.

For a while.

Then Barnaby noticed that he'd gained a few pounds. He noticed that almost everyone he saw had gained weight. Worse, everyone smelled. Very few bars of soap escaped the Transubstantiator. Very few folks took showers or baths anymore.

"I'd better do something about this," Barnaby told Myra.

"Mmffff," Myra said, trying to speak with her mouth full of candy.

Barnaby got to work and came up with the perfect conversion strategy. He constructed a modified model of the Transubstantiator. As the word spread, people flocked to his home, eager to see what he'd done.

"Watch," Barnaby said when he'd tightened the final bolt and was ready to test his invention. He struggled to lift the old tire he'd found behind the garage and put it in his new machine. Then he pressed a button.

The new machine sprang into action, chugging and huffing and making a wide assortment of sounds normally associated with a washing machine that is about to burst into flame. When all was still again, Barnaby reached inside and pulled out an armful of soap, neatly cut into perfectly shaped bars. That had been the hardest part of his new invention—getting the bars cut so neatly—and he was really proud of how well it worked.

"Soap," Barnaby said.

"Soap!" the crowd shouted. "Yay!" They rushed forward and grabbed all the bars. *I did it,* Barnaby thought as he posted the modification plans on his website.

He was happy for the rest of the day. The next day, he learned that the people put all the soap they'd taken into their Transubstantiators. They didn't wash. They made more candy.

The people grew so fat and stinky that nobody ever invited them to visit. Not that it mattered. Since they didn't have any tires for their cars, they couldn't go anywhere, even if they wanted to.

"I've got it," Barnaby told Myra after a full week of brainstorming. "I've figured out how to turn chairs into tires."

"Oh boy," Myra said.

Barnaby hurried to the garage to start looking for parts.

Myra hurried into the kitchen to find a chair to sit on. She realized it might be her last chance.

ROADWORK

The road crew was working at the end of Jacob's street. He saw them when he left his house each morning to go to school—five guys wearing ragged jeans, faded flannel shirts, orange vests, and yellow hard hats. He saw them when he came home. Sometimes, a cement truck would be sitting there. Sometimes, an asphalt truck. Once every two or three days, Jacob heard a jackhammer while he was doing his homework. But mostly, the whole crew just seemed to be standing around, or sitting on the open tailgate of a truck.

"Nice job," Jacob muttered as he left for school. "They get paid to stand there."

His house was the next-to-last one on the street. The crew was at the very end of the road. Jacob knew the road was going to be extended eventually, to connect with the other side of the development. At the rate the crew was going, Jacob figured they were adding about a yard a week. It looked like they'd be there forever.

Saturday morning, he decided to walk down and see what was going on. As he approached, nobody even looked at him. One guy was holding a shovel, pushing around a small pile of gravel the way a little kid would push around a plateful of peas he didn't want to eat. Two of the others were sitting on the back of the pickup truck, drinking coffee from paper cups. The other two were leaning against the truck.

"What are you doing?" Jacob asked.

The guy with the shovel looked over at him. He had a shaggy beard that brushed the collar of his shirt. "What's it look like we're doing?"

"Nothing," Jacob said.

"It might look that way," one of the guys on the truck said. "But this is very special work. Most roads don't last long. They get cracks and potholes. Ours are built to last. We guarantee them."

"How can you do that?" Jacob asked. He'd seen trucks all over town fixing the roads. He knew that the roads started to break down right after they were built. They got really bad in the winter.

"We've discovered long-lost secrets," the guy with the shovel said. "We studied road building throughout history, all the way back to ancient Rome and beyond, and all around the world, from Ireland to Ecuador. We've hunted down ancient manuscripts and lost scrolls."

"And the secret is sitting around drinking coffee?" Jacob asked. He was enjoying himself. He didn't get many chances to make fun of adults.

The man with the shovel shook his head. "No. That's not the secret. And we aren't sitting around."

"It sure looks to me like you're sitting around," Jacob said. "What a great job. Sit around, stare at the sky, drink coffee, and get paid."

The guy with the shovel stepped away from the gravel pile. "No. It might look that way. But what we're really doing isn't just sitting around. We're waiting."

"Waiting for what?" Jacob asked.

The guy didn't answer him right away. Instead, he looked over at the rest of the crew. They nodded, as if agreeing with some unspoken questions.

"Come on, tell me," Jacob said. "What are you waiting for?"

"A sacrifice," the guy with the shovel said. "That's the secret. For a road to last, it requires a sacrifice." He lifted the shovel over his shoulder.

At first, Jacob didn't understand what he meant—not until the shovel was swinging toward his head. And by then, by the time he understood, he really didn't care how long the road would last. But he realized whether the road lasted a day or a century, it would outlast him.

FINDER*S* LO*S*ER*S*

What's that?" Maddie pointed up to the second-floor window of Oliver's house as he came out to join her. She and the other kids had stopped there on the way to the ball field. "It looks like a trapped bird."

Oliver squinted against the sunlight and shaded his eyes with his hand. "I think it's that tot-finder thing."

"Oh yeah, I have one on my window," Maddie said. She could barely remember when the sticker was bright red. After years of sitting in the sun, all the color had faded, leaving the sticker a dull silver, like the one on Oliver's window.

"I got one, too," Brad said.

Katie and Sarah nodded. So did Stan.

"What's it for?" Nolan asked.

Maddie stared at him. "Don't you have one?"

Nolan shrugged. "I don't know."

"It's for firemen and stuff like that," Oliver said. "So they can find you if there's an emergency."

"I guess your parents don't care about you," Brad said.

"That's not true," Nolan said. "I'll bet I have a sticker."

"Let's go," Maddie said. As she turned away from Oliver's house, a glittering flash caught her eye. "Hey, it came off."

She watched the tot-finder sticker flutter to the roof of Oliver's porch.

"They're supposed to stick forever," Katie said.

"I guess your sticker is defective, Oliver," Brad said. "Just like you."

"Shut up," Oliver said. "There's nothing wrong with it. And they don't have to stick on forever. They just have to stick while we're little."

"This is stupid," Maddie said. "Who cares about the sticker? So what if it's a cheap one? Let's play ball."

"It's not defective," Oliver said again. "I'll prove it." He grabbed one of the supports on the side of the porch and started to climb to the top.

Maddie watched as he pulled himself onto the roof. "Got it," he said, holding up the sticker. He started to climb back down, but slipped at the edge of the roof.

Maddie let out a scream as Oliver fell. Oliver let out a grunt as he hit the ground. Everyone else ran over to him. Maddie waited to see if there'd be blood. She had no idea what to do to help someone who'd been in an accident. Whenever anyone got hurt, her first instinct was to run away.

Luckily, Oliver sat up, still holding the sticker.

"You okay?" Nolan asked.

"I think so." Oliver got to his feet. "See, there's nothing wrong with it. The glue just dried out."

"It isn't supposed to dry out," Katie said.

"Oh yeah? Let's check yours, then," Oliver said.

They headed down the street to Katie's house. When they got there, Oliver pointed at a window on the first floor. "Yours is coming off, too."

"Just a little," Katie said. "It's only a tiny corner."

"I'll bet it's loose." Nolan grabbed the corner and pulled. The whole sticker came off.

"You ripped it," Katie said. She snatched the sticker from Nolan.

Maddie saw there was a tear in one side of the sticker, right through the leg of the child in the picture. "So what!" she yelled. "It's a stupid sticker. We don't even need them anymore. We're not babies. Let's just go play ball! Okay?"

"We never needed them," Nolan said. "There's never been a fire around here."

"Yeah, there was," Maddie said. She pointed down the road. "We were really little. A chemical truck came around the curve too fast and hit that house."

"Yeah," Oliver said. "My dad took some pictures. He's always shouting at the trucks. They aren't supposed to come through here."

"Mine shout at them, too," Maddie said. Their street was between two busy highways. A sign at each end read:

NO TRUCKS. "But who cares? Come on, can we please go play ball now?"

They headed to the ball field. But on the way, Nolan stopped at his house. "Hey, I was wrong. I have one, too. I guess I never paid any attention to it."

His sticker was loose, too. Oliver went over and pulled it off the window, rolling it into a tight tube. "You mind?" he asked Nolan.

"Nope. I'm not a tot," Nolan said.

And then, finally, they got to the ball field, where they met up with the rest of their friends.

In the first inning, trying to slide into second base, Katie cut her leg on a stone.

This time, there was blood.

"I think you might need stitches," Maddie said, backing away and hoping someone else would step in.

"I'll walk you home," Sarah said.

She and Katie left.

In the second inning, Nolan caught a line drive with his stomach. He dropped to the ground and curled up.

As Maddie stood off to the side, it hit her. "Oh, no!"

"What?" Oliver asked.

She pointed at him. "Your sticker fell. Then you fell. Right?"

"Yeah. So?"

"And then Katie," Maddie said. "Her sticker's leg was torn. Then she cut her leg. And you rolled up Nolan's sticker. Now look at him. He's all rolled up, too."

Maddie thought about her own sticker. Was it loose?

Could it fall soon and get stepped on or blown down the street? She knew what she had to do—peel it off carefully and put it somewhere safe. "I gotta go."

She headed off the field. Oliver followed her.

"What are you doing?" she asked.

"Oh, nothing." He sped up and moved past her.

"Liar. You're going to do something to my sticker," Maddie said.

He glanced over his shoulder. "No, I'm not."

But she could tell, from his grin, that this was exactly what he had in mind. And it would be something bad. Maybe he'd rip the head off, or tear it in half. She had to stop him.

Oliver dashed off. Maddie grabbed her baseball, then chased after him. He was faster than Maddie, but not by much. Luckily, she looked before she crossed the street near her house. A milk truck was barreling past. She almost ran right in front of it. She wasn't the only one who had a close call. If the driver hadn't hit his brakes, Oliver would have been flattened.

She got to her house seconds after Oliver. She saw him running for the backyard. Her bedroom was in the rear, on the first floor. She followed him.

Her sticker was just starting to peel. Oliver reached for it.

"Stop!" Maddie screamed.

Oliver ignored her. He grabbed the end of the sticker.

"No!" Maddie hurled the ball at him, aiming right for his shoulder. *He deserves to get hit,* she thought.

Oliver ducked. The ball smacked the window, right on the sticker. The whole window shattered.

Maddie froze for an instant. Then she heard her father shout, "What was that?"

"Run!" Oliver raced out of the backyard.

Maddie wanted to flee, but she had to see what happened to the sticker. She went to the window, stood on her toes, and looked inside. Shards of glass littered her bedroom floor. Some of them were covered with small pieces of the tot-finder sticker. The sticker wasn't just torn; it was totally shattered.

Maddie heard her parents coming down the hallway. She fled from the yard, wondering whether she'd shatter, too.

No way, she thought as she reached the sidewalk. A kid could fall or get cut. A kid could crumple. But there was no way a kid could shatter.

"I'll be okay," she gasped. "Maybe I'll get a cut or scratch, or I'll get hit by a baseball, but that's got to be all."

The front door flew open. Her father came onto the steps. Maddie raced across the street.

She heard a screech of tires. A car was hurtling right toward her. Maddie froze. She was too terrified to save herself. But some small part of her brain told her—*This isn't your fate. The car can't shatter you.* In a weird way, she felt safe.

The small voice was right. The car swerved. It didn't hit Maddie. Instead, it shot past her and slammed into the cab of a truck that was speeding the other way down the street. The truck jackknifed, and the cargo tipped. Maddie tried to leap back. The giant silver tanker smashed down right in front of her. She read the sideways lettering. DANGER. LIQUID NITROGEN.

The tanker burst open.

Liquid nitrogen.

Maddie remembered when her science teacher had stuck a tennis ball in a beaker of liquid nitrogen and then hit it with a hammer. The ball was frozen so solid, it had shattered.

Shattered. Like the sticker.

Behind her, Maddie heard the screech of more tires. She froze, too scared to move. She knew this car would hit her. But not quite yet. Not while she still had a chance to survive the impact in one piece. It wouldn't hit her until it could shatter her.

The flood of spilled liquid nitrogen reached her. As the stunningly cold liquid splashed over Maddie, she froze again. For real.

CLOUDY WITH A CHANCE OF MESSAGE

Janet was walking home from school when she saw it. There was no mistake. It wasn't her imagination. It wasn't something that might or might not be, like the animal faces she sometimes imagined she saw in the swirling grain of a piece of wood. This was definitely real. There, in the clouds, was a perfect image of the letter *T*.

This means something, Janet thought as she stood gazing into the sky. The *T*, a pure white piece of cloud with unnaturally straight edges, stayed together for a long time, then slowly drifted into formless fluff.

What can it stand for? Janet wondered. Surely, this was a message with deep meaning. Maybe it was even something that would change her life.

As she walked home, she tried to find an answer. She had no close friends whose first or last name began with a *T*. There was Tanya Wirth, who sat two seats away from her in class, and Bill Trixton, who sat in the back of the room. But she really didn't hang out with either of them.

Maybe it isn't a person. Janet was suddenly sure it was a word. But what word?

"Tree?" she whispered.

No, all the trees along the block were new and small, barely more than saplings. There was nothing good or bad they would do to her.

"Trumpet?"

She'd never even seen one close up.

"Tarantula?"

There weren't any around here.

"Taco . . . tennis . . . tablecloth? . . ."

Nothing seemed to fit. *Maybe I should just forget about it.*

Just then, she saw another *T* in the clouds, as perfect and undeniable as the first one. She stood and watched until this letter, too, drifted apart.

That was enough to convince her that this was a special message. There was only one thing to do. The very thought of it made her cringe. It was a huge task, but she had to do it. As soon as she got home, she'd get the dictionary and look at every word that began with the letter *T*. The answer would be there. It had to be. Janet was sure of that. And she was sure she'd know it when she saw it.

Janet ran the rest of the way home. Before she got there, she saw a third *T* form in the clouds. This could definitely be the most important message in her whole life, but only if she managed to figure it out.

When she got home, she went straight to the living room and looked in the bookcase. But the dictionary wasn't there. Janet ran into the kitchen. "Mom, where's the dictionary?"

"I think it's in your brother's room," her mom said. "But what's the rush? Sit down and relax for a minute. Come on." She held up a box that said ORANGE-LEMON SPICE. "Join me for a nice, quiet cup of tea."

"No time," Janet said.

"No time for a nice, relaxing cup of tea?" her mom asked.

"Maybe later," Janet said. Right now, she had to find the answer to that mysterious message from the clouds. What was the meaning of that letter? She ran out of the kitchen and headed for the stairs. There was no way she could relax until she figured out the message.

Behind her, the teakettle blew out a steamy cloud and whistled a high-pitched laugh.

FAMILY TIME

Stephen had just finished clearing the table and was about to sneak off to his room for a few hours of mindless video games when his mom snagged him with those horrible words.

"Stephen," she said, "it's Thursday. You know what we do on Thursday."

Stephen stopped in his tracks. *Here it comes,* he thought.

"Family time!" his little sister, Tiffany, shouted. "Thursday is family time," she said through a mouth missing more than a few teeth.

"What will it be?" his dad asked. "A board game, a word game, or a card game?"

"Board game," Stephen said, hoping to keep the damage to a minimum. At least he could handle something like Scrabble or Parcheesi. That would be bearable.

"Cards!" everyone else shouted.

"Cards it is," his dad said. "I'll get the deck."

"Can we play Crazy Eights?" Stephen asked. "That's a fun game. Or how about Go Fish?" *Please*, he thought, *please play something normal.*

"No!" Tiffany shouted. "I want to play double-deck wangle."

Stephen cringed at those words.

"Yes, wangle," his mother agreed.

"Wangle it is," his dad said, returning with two decks of cards, a pad of paper, a pencil, and a real big grin.

"But . . ." Stephen's mind frantically searched for any words, any excuses or suggestions or ideas that could stop what was about to happen. He failed.

They sat at the table. Stephen's dad handed the deck to Stephen's mom. "You cut them, Betty."

She cut the cards. "Oh good, a seven of hearts." She held the red-spotted card up for all to admire. She seemed pleased. "That means it's your deal, Tiffany."

"Goody," Tiffany said.

Stephen didn't have any idea how the seven of hearts meant that his sister got the first deal. He didn't bother asking—he knew he wouldn't understand the answer.

Tiffany shuffled the double decks, then dealt out the cards. Each person got three cards facedown, then two more faceup. Then each got three more, but some were up and some were down. Stephen didn't understand the reason for any of it.

"I've got proof of trump," his father said. "That gives me the first play." He put down a card.

"Reflux aggressive," his mom said, placing three cards on the table.

"Tribbly scoop," Tiffany said, picking up one card from the table and putting down another.

Stephen had sat through this scene a thousand times during family hour, and he still had no idea what was going on. He realized everyone was looking at him. He reached for one of the cards on the table.

"Steph," his father said, "you know you can't borgy until there are three bleats played."

"Uh, yeah, sorry. I forgot." He jerked his hand back, then tossed down a card from those he held.

"Nice reverse triskum," his mom said.

Stephen relaxed slightly.

"Come on," Tiffany said, "a two-year-old could have made that move. He had a perfect chance for an angry fleebax with the nine of diamonds and the five of spades, but he didn't even see it. It's like he doesn't even know what he's doing." She grinned at him, looking like some sort of Halloween pumpkin carved by a lunatic dentist.

"Now, Tiffany, that's not nice," her mom said. "Your play, dear," she said to Stephen's dad.

"Indeed." He looked at the cards in his hand, then down at the cards on the table. "Got to try a navux," he said, picking a card off the top of the deck. His face broke into a giant grin. "Well, lookee here, aren't I lucky tonight." He held up a three of clubs. "Triple slimper on a two-way bixley. That's a relief. I was so sure I'd get skidinkled." He placed the three on top of a king of diamonds that was on the table, then covered them both with a jack of diamonds.

"Very nice, dear," Stephen's mom said.

"Good play, Dad," Tiffany told him.

"Uh, nice move," Stephen said. In all too short a time, it was his turn again. They all looked at him like they were expecting something special. He reached toward one of the cards on the table. Their smiles started to disappear. He pulled his hand back. They waited. He reached for one of his faceup cards. They didn't lose their smiles. He pulled out the card and put it in the center of the table.

"Nice royal flixum," his mom said.

"Thanks." Stephen checked the clock on the wall. It was almost over. Family hour was nearly done for the week. He'd survived again.

"Aren't you going to box the end leapers?" Tiffany asked, giving him that silly gloating grin again.

"Huh?"

"The end leapers." She reached over, picked up his card, and turned it sideways. "Forty more points that way," she said.

"Thanks." Stephen stared at the table. From what he saw, the cards might as well have been shaken up in a bag and tossed out by the handful. None of it meant anything.

"This is nice," his dad said. "I'm glad we can all get together for family fun."

"Me, too," his mom agreed. "It's so nice that we have this time together. Don't you think so, kids?"

"Yeah," Tiffany said.

"You like it, too, don't you, Steph?" his mom asked.

Stephen knew this was his chance. He wanted to throw the stupid cards across the room and shout, *"I don't understand any of this!"* He wanted to tell them he had no idea what was going on, that he'd never had any idea, and he doubted he ever would have any idea. They'd explained, they'd showed examples, they'd told him over and over. He just didn't get it.

"It's his favorite," his dad said. "It's everyone's favorite, right, Steph?"

"Sure," Stephen said. "I love it."

"I've got an idea," his mom said. "Since we're having so much fun, why stop? There's no rule that says family hour has to be only sixty minutes. Let's play for another hour. Is that okay with everyone?"

"Great," his dad said.

"Yay!" Tiffany screamed.

"No," Stephen said. He wasn't even sure if he'd spoken aloud or just thought the word. It didn't matter. They couldn't possibly hear him over their shouts of joy.

GEE! OGRAPHY

This is a real pain," Eric whispered as he took a spot at the end of the line behind Darren.

"Yeah, but it will be over really fast," Darren said.

"Especially for me." Eric figured he'd be booted out of the geography bee quicker than a turtle in a dodgeball game. That was fine. He'd be happy to sit at his desk and watch the rest of the class struggle with unpronounceable world capitals, unmemorizable river names, and far too many majestic mountain ranges. Right now, the kids were all standing along the side of the room by the windows, waiting for Mr. Bedecker to start asking questions.

Eric glanced toward the front of the line. Bobby the Brain was the first one there, looking eager to show everyone how smart he was. And Cindy Merkle, who once actually brought her globe in from home for show and tell, was right behind him, followed by Tracey Orben and Kim Fletcher.

"You can tell who likes geography," Eric whispered to Darren.

"Let's all pay attention," Mr. Bedecker said. "We're ready to begin. Take your time. Think about your answer. Remember, the three winners from our class get to compete in the school contest. The first-place winner in our class gets a small prize, too." He held up a bag of gummi worms.

Eric loved gummi worms, but he was pretty sure he'd lose on the first round. He liked math and science, and he loved reading, but geography was hard. He just wasn't good at memorizing facts. He waited for his moment of doom as the line moved toward Mr. Bedecker.

Darren's turn came.

"Name a state that borders Canada," Mr. Bedecker said.

Eric couldn't believe his friend's luck. That had to be the easiest question he'd heard so far.

"Oregon," Darren said. "No, wait!" He closed his eyes, as if looking at a map. "I mean, Washington."

"Right," Mr. Bedecker said.

Darren let out a sigh of relief and walked to the end of the line. It was Eric's turn.

"Ready, Eric?" Mr. Bedecker asked.

"I guess."

Mr. Bedecker read the question. "Name a country on the Arabian peninsula along the Strait of Hormuz."

Oh, man, he's got to be kidding, Eric thought. This was so unfair, especially after Darren's easy question. Eric had heard of Arabia, but the rest of the question was gibberish. *Oh, man, I'm really going to look stupid.* He was so lost, he couldn't even dream up a wild guess. When he opened his mouth, all that came out was, "Oh, man."

Mr. Bedecker stared at Eric for a moment. Then he stared at the sheet of paper in his hand. Then he stared back at Eric. *No gummi worms for me,* Eric thought as his head slumped in defeat.

Before Eric could leave the line and slink back to his desk, Mr Bedecker smiled. "Very good. You're absolutely right. The Sultantate of Oman is correct."

"Wow," Darren whispered when Eric stepped up behind him. "How'd you know that? I'd never even heard of Oman."

"Not a clue," Eric whispered back. He couldn't believe he'd gotten so lucky. He watched as a bunch of kids, including Darren, were knocked out in the second round. Then Mr. Bedecker asked Eric, "Can you name the country whose capital is Oslo?"

"No way," Eric blurted out.

"Correct again, Eric," Mr. Bedecker said. "Norway is the right answer."

Eric was so stunned, and the line of remaining kids was so short, he was caught by surprise when his third turn came around.

"Well, Eric?" Mr. Bedecker asked.

Eric stared at him. He had no idea what the question was.

"Eric, please don't tell me you weren't paying attention," Mr. Bedecker said.

All Eric could do was mutter, "Sorry."

Mr. Bedecker looked even more surprised than before. "Very, very good, Eric. I owe you an apology. I see you were definitely paying attention. Runnymede and Epsom are both in the English county of Surrey. I had no idea you were such a serious student of geography. Even I wasn't sure about that one until I checked my textbook."

Eric looked at Darren and shrugged. Then he looked at the line. It wasn't much of a line anymore. It was just four other kids. He'd almost made it into the top three.

His next turn came quickly. "What is the capital of Macau?"

"Macau?" Eric had never even heard of that place.

Mr. Bedecker nodded. "Correct. Macau is the name of the capital city as well as the country."

Two more kids got knocked out. Eric had made it to the final three. All of them would compete in the school contest. But first, they'd see who was the winner for the class and, more important, the winner of those gummi worms.

"The rules get stricter now," Mr. Bedecker said. "No second chances. Make sure of your answer before you speak. Does everyone understand?"

"Yes." Eric didn't care if they changed the rules. *It doesn't matter. I can't lose*, he thought. *I can say anything and I'll be right.* Somehow, he was riding a lucky streak. He'd seen it happen in sports and on game shows. No reason it couldn't happen during a geography bee. He was invincible. Invulnerable. Unbeatable. He couldn't wait to nail the question.

Eric pushed his tongue against the side of his left rear molar, as if already prying away stuck bits of gummi worm. The bag was as good as his. *Give me your toughest question.* He'd never won anything in his whole life, and he was really enjoying how good it felt to be a champ.

Mr. Bedecker glanced down at the sheet of questions, then nodded, as if he, too, realized that Eric would know the answer. "What is the name of the country that is directly south of the United States?"

Eric barely listened. "Yummy gummi mummy tummy," he blurted out, confident that anything he said would be correct. Half a second later, it sank in what he'd just done. "Wait. Mexico! I mean Mexico. I know that. Everyone knows that."

"I'm sorry, Eric. You heard the rules. I have to take your first answer," Mr. Bedecker said. "I regret to inform you that 'yummy gummi mummy tummy' is not a country directly south of the United States. Or anywhere else, as far as I know."

"But . . ." Eric stood for a moment, waiting for his luck to return, then shuffled over to his desk as the imagined taste of gummi worms faded from his mouth. He sat and watched Cindy win first place, with Bobby coming in second. The bell rang. School was over for the day.

"Come on," Darren said. "Let's go hang out at my house."

"I can't," Eric said.

"Why not?"

Eric picked up his geography book. "I have to study for

the school contest. I only have one week, and there's a ton of stuff to learn."

"Study? You're kidding," Darren said.

Eric shook his head. "Nope, I'm serious. I have to get ready. There's a lot more to winning than just luck, you know."

THE SPIDER SHOUTER

Kill it!" Roger shouted. He pointed at the spider that sat like a small plum in the center of the huge web. "I hate them."

"They're kind of cool." Dana walked over toward the corner of the porch and studied the web. "I like spiders."

"I don't," Roger said. "They creep me out. They look all swollen in back, like they're filled with green icky stuff."

"Chill out." Dana thought the spider was awesome. Not that she'd want one crawling on her or anything like that. She felt Roger, who'd come over from next door to borrow a magazine, was way too nervous about everything. "It won't hurt you."

"Go away!" Roger shouted at the spider.

The spider skittered to the side of the web near the house.

"Hey, it listened to you," Dana said.

"No way," Roger said. "Spiders don't have ears."

"Sure they do. Everything has ears." But even as she said that, she realized she wasn't sure.

"Bacteria don't have ears," Roger said.

"I'm talking about animals and bugs and stuff," Dana said.

"Well, bugs don't have ears. I'll prove it." Roger stepped closer to the web—but not too close—and shouted, "Get off the porch!"

The spider dropped down from the web. Dana saw that it was dangling from a tiny glistening line of spider silk. When the spider reached the floor of the porch, it ran to the edge and went over the side.

"It totally heard you," Dana said.

"No way." Roger shook his head.

"Come on. I'm looking this up." Dana ran inside. She was going to check out the answer online, but on the way to her room, she passed her parents' bookcase with the old encyclopedia. She grabbed the volume for the letter S and opened it to the page for spiders.

She skimmed the subject lines until she saw "Senses."

"Okay, here it is. They don't have ears. . . ."

"Told you." Roger smirked.

"But they sort of hear. They feel vibrations in their legs. So it felt what you said." She held up the page to show Roger. "Try calling it."

"That's stupid. There's no way the spider listened to me. I'll prove it."

Roger went back outside. Dana followed him to the porch.

"Here, spider!" Roger yelled, like he was calling a dog. "Come here, spider. Hey, spider. Come here."

Dana watched the porch boards beneath the web. For a moment, nothing happened.

Then the spider crawled into sight. It didn't climb back to the web. Instead, it raced right toward Roger with eight tiny legs pumping like it was desperate to reach him.

"Ahhhgg!" Roger ran to the other side of the porch. The spider followed him.

"Ahhg!" he screamed again when he reached the railing. He stomped down on the spider.

"Why'd you do that?" Dana asked. "Spiders are good." She pointed to another paragraph in the encyclopedia. "It says they help control bad insects."

"I don't care. I don't want one chasing after me," Roger said. "You shouldn't have told me to call it."

"Oh, now you're blaming me? You're the one who called it." Before Dana could say anything else, a motion to her side caught her attention. Another spider, just as large as the first one, was coming up from the front of the porch.

She watched as it ran toward Roger. She wasn't sure whether to warn him. She didn't want the spider to get stomped, but she didn't think Roger would want the spider crawling on him. She pointed.

"Arggg!" Roger shouted and stomped.

A third spider came from under the porch. And then a fourth.

Roger stomped them both. He let out a howl of anger

and fear. But the sound suddenly cut off. Roger grabbed his throat. He moved his lips. A faint whisper came out.

Dana had seen that happen once before. Her father had shouted so loudly at an umpire during a softball game that he'd lost his voice. He hadn't been able to speak above a whisper for three days after that.

Dana saw another spider coming toward them. This one was on the sidewalk, near the front steps.

"Go away!" she shouted.

The spider kept coming. Dana realized it wasn't listening to her. "You tell it," she said to Roger.

"Go away!" Roger's words, dribbling from his injured throat, barely reached Dana's ears. The spider didn't slow down.

"I guess they don't listen to whispers," Dana said.

Roger stomped two more spiders that had reached the porch. He pointed to the lawn and whispered, "There can't be that many more."

Dana glanced at the encyclopedia. At the bottom of the page, above the last paragraph, she saw the heading "Spider Population."

The edge of the lawn by the sidewalk rippled like the surface of a lake when the breeze kicks up. Spiders were moving over it, bending the blades of grass as they traveled. Lots of spiders.

"We'll stomp them all," Roger whispered.

Dana shook her head.

"How many?" he asked.

Dana read the last sentence out loud: "Even in a town

or city, there can be more than a million spiders in every acre."

The whole lawn rippled. Dana turned toward the house, but spiders were coming down the walls now, and covering the door. In a moment, they were covering her and Roger like a living coat of brown and black paint.

Roger's shout was more a gasp than a whisper now.

Dana's scream was louder. But it didn't last very long.

THE PYRAMID MAN

There came to the village of Meander a man dressed as a merchant. He wore not the poor clothes of a tinker or peddler, but the rich garb of one who sold silk or silver.

But he bore no such common wares.

The merchant, who spoke not a word, strode through town holding aloft a small pyramid of painted wood. Each triangular side was a different color.

"What's that?" a boy asked.

The merchant smiled and held his hand a bit higher, as if the sight of the item itself were sufficient answer, but still didn't speak.

The boy followed the merchant. Another boy and a girl joined the procession, along with several adults. Soon, all who saw were following, for there was little enough to break the tedium of the day, and this stranger was obviously no ordinary traveler.

"What is it?" one man asked.

"What does it do?" asked another.

But the merchant responded to none of these questions. Holding the pyramid at chest level in his open palm, he continued to walk at the same steady pace. The people followed. Eventually, after circling the village, he reached his wagon where he'd left it, near the edge of a cow pasture. There, standing on a tree stump, he spoke.

"Good villagers, I bring you an amazing offer." He pointed to the burlap sacks piled in a rough pyramid of their own in the back of his wagon. "Each sack holds one hundred of these wonderful items. For you good people, since you strike me as honest and hardworking, I will sell a whole sack for the small price of two silver coins."

"But what would we want with them?" an elder from the village asked.

"Don't you see?" the merchant said. "As I am selling them to you, you may sell them to others. Listen carefully, for here is the beauty of it all—you may charge more than you paid, and thus make a handsome profit. Sell a sack for three silver coins, and you'll earn a coin for every sack you sell. Or sell half a sack for two coins, and make an even larger profit."

"But why would anyone buy the pyramids from us?" a man asked.

"So that they may then also sell them to others," the merchant said. "Fear not of getting all you need—when you have sold as many pyramids as you can carry, return to me and I will provide more. We can all be rich as kings. Every one of us will gain great wealth."

He paused.

In the silence, one could hear the idea take hold as man after man and woman after woman imagined a road to riches contained in the sacks piled upon the wagon.

The villagers bought every sack the merchant had in his wagon and soon scattered to the four corners of the land. And these sacks they did sell to others, who did sell them to still others.

The merchant grew rich as a king. Those who bought his pyramids and sold them to others grew rich as princes. And those who bought from them and sold to still others grew rich as dukes. And those who bought from them grew slightly richer. But those who bought next soon found that every man in the land was also selling pyramids. There were no buyers left.

Those who had come late to this wonderful plan went to see the merchant and complain, dragging their full sacks and hoping for their money back. But the merchant, who had become the richest one of all, had already sailed toward other lands far away across the sea, where he could again sell pyramids to the greedy and the foolish.

WALK THE DOG

Priscilla, I need a favor," Mrs. Grutcheon said.

Priscilla stood at the door, wondering what her neighbor wanted this time. "I'm doing my homework."

"Well, that's perfect," Mrs. Grutcheon said. "You can do it at my house. I just need someone to watch Boopsie this afternoon while I go help my sister make pies for the bake sale."

"I'm really kind of busy," Priscilla said. She didn't want to spend the afternoon cooped up in her neighbor's house with her neighbor's dog.

"I keep three video game consoles for when my grandchildren visit, I have all the newest movies, and I just bought a machine that makes milk shakes," Mrs. Grutcheon said. "You can hang out, play some games, do your homework, have some snacks. And I'll pay you for your time. Please?"

Priscilla let out a loud and long sigh, just to show what

a large imposition all of this was. Still, money was money, and milk shakes were wonderful. "Okay. I'll do it."

"Splendid." Mrs. Grutcheon clapped her hands together like she was killing a mosquito. "Boopsie will be thrilled to have your company."

"I'll bet," Priscilla muttered. She started to follow Mrs. Grutcheon next door.

"Don't you want to bring your homework?" Mrs. Grutcheon asked.

"No. I'll finish it later." Actually, there wasn't any homework, but Priscilla didn't think she needed to reveal that.

When they reached Mrs. Grutcheon's house, Boopsie came charging over, yapping and vibrating. She sniffed Priscilla's feet and then started licking her toes. Priscilla wished she hadn't worn sandals.

"Oh, look at that," Mrs. Grutcheon said. "How sweet. She really likes you."

She gave Priscilla a quick tour of the house, explained the TV remote, and showed her how to make milk shakes. Then, as she grabbed her coat, she pointed to a leash hanging from a hook by the front door. "I already fed Boopsie. She'll probably nap for a while. Take her out when she wants to go. That's all you really have to do."

"How will I know when she wants to go?" Priscilla asked.

"You'll know. Boopsie is very good at expressing her needs."

Mrs. Grutcheon left. Priscilla went into the kitchen to

make a strawberry milk shake. Boopsie followed her. "Leave me alone," Priscilla said.

Boopsie sat, stared at Priscilla, and panted.

Priscilla took her milk shake into the living room and switched on the TV. She wasn't in the mood to play a video game, so she looked through the movies in the bookcase and found one she hadn't seen. Boopsie ran around for a while, sniffed things, chewed other things, then finally curled up near Priscilla's feet and went to sleep.

"This definitely works for me," Priscilla said.

One and a half movies and three milk shakes later, Boopsie woke up. She ran to the front door and whined. Then she put her front paws on the wall right under the leash. She ran back to Priscilla and barked.

"Shhh, this is the good part," Priscilla said.

Boopsie paced around and whined some more. Priscilla ignored her.

The movie ended. Prisicilla got up from the couch. Boopsie raced for the door.

Priscilla went back to the kitchen. *One more milk shake,* she thought.

Boopsie ran after her. When Priscilla reached the living room, she noticed another stack of movies on a table next to the couch. One of the boxes caught her eye. "My favorite!" she said. She sat, drank her milk shake, and started watching the movie.

Boopsie whined louder.

"Stop it!" Priscilla shouted.

Boopsie ran to the front door and scratched at it. Priscilla ignored her.

Toward the end of the movie, Priscilla realized she needed to go to the bathroom. She got up from the couch.

Boopsie sprang to her feet and ran in circles around her. "I told you, leave me alone!" Priscilla said. She walked down the hall to the bathroom.

Boopsie raced past her, reached the door first, and spun around. She stood in the doorway and growled.

"Hey!" Priscilla said. She backed up a step. "Let me in."

Boopsie stood her ground. She was small, but she looked like she could do some serious damage.

Priscilla walked back down the hall. She knew there had to be at least one more bathroom in the house. She went upstairs. Yeah—there was one at the end of the hallway. She headed for it.

Boopsie got there first and guarded the door.

"That's it. I'm going home," she said.

She went downstairs.

Boopsie blocked the front door.

Priscilla reached for the knob. Boopsie growled. Priscilla reached for the leash. Boopsie stopped growling.

Priscilla grabbed the leash, hooked one end to Boopsie's collar, and opened the door.

"Hurry up," she said as the dog tugged her down the porch steps. Priscilla waited while the dog went to the bathroom.

"My turn," she said as she tugged at the leash. "Hurry up." She got inside and dashed for the bathroom. She almost made it. But four milk shakes means a lot of liquid.

Maybe I can blame the dog, she thought as she stared at the wet spot in the hallway carpet.

Behind her, Boopsie growled.

"Guess not," Priscilla muttered as she headed to the kitchen in search of cleaning supplies.

Boopsie hopped up on the couch and settled down. This was one of her favorites movies, too.

WARM RAIN

Pair up, class."

"Now?" That caught me by surprise. We weren't even inside the museum yet.

"Now," Mrs. Kimmel said.

Everyone was running around the parking lot like this was the World Series of musical chairs and the music had just stopped. I spun toward my friend Marcus. But Gabriel beat me to it.

"Can we do groups of three?" I called to Mrs. Kimmel.

"*Pair* up," she said, shooting me that annoyed look she gets whenever I ask a question.

I searched the crowd, hoping to spot someone I could stand to be stuck with for the next three hours. The good choices were rapidly vanishing. I don't do well under pressure. I like to take my time and think about things before I make a decision.

Daryl Hostner wasn't paired up yet. He was okay. It

would be nice if he changed his shirt a bit more often, but the smell wasn't all that bad yet, since it was only Wednesday. I headed toward him. I was halfway there when he teamed up with Collin Anderson.

The situation was starting to stink worse than Daryl. Everyone had a partner. Wait. That would work. If there was nobody for me, then Mrs. Kimmel would have to let me go with Marcus and Gabriel. Or by myself, which would be just fine, too. I knew exactly what I wanted to see.

"Looks like it's you and me."

I turned toward the voice. Oh no. Toby Praxton. Toby the Talker.

There had to be another choice. I spotted two other lone figures—Larissa Caliban, who was in a ten-second TV commercial once and has been unbearable ever since, and Dan Weft, who sprayed everything within five feet of him whenever he talked.

"Yeah, I guess it's you and me. That's outstanding." Toby held up a folder crammed with papers. "You know what? You're in luck. I downloaded the museum guide last week. Then I researched every single exhibit. I'm all set. I know all the best displays. This is going to be an unforgettable experience."

I'll bet.

Following Mrs. Kimmel like hyperactive ducklings, our class streamed into the museum through the side entrance reserved for mobs of kids.

"I even made a map," Toby said. "That way, we won't

risk missing anything. I figured we'd be asked to pair up, so I printed an extra copy for my partner. It's laminated." He shoved a stiff sheet of plastic-coated paper into my hand. "You must be feeling pretty lucky to have gotten me before anyone else."

"I definitely can't believe my luck," I said.

"Meet back here at twelve fifteen," Mrs. Kimmel called over the noise of our escape.

Gabriel and Marcus were already racing toward the dinosaurs. I started to walk that way.

"Where are you going?" Toby asked.

I pointed to the left. "Dinosaurs."

"No, that's completely wrong. We need to go through the basement first. See, it's all marked here on the map. I even time-coded it."

"Don't you like dinosaurs?"

Toby nodded. "Sure. Don't worry. We won't miss anything. That's the brilliance of my system." He glanced at his map. "I've scheduled the triceratops for eleven thirty-seven."

"Triceratops? You mean stegosaurus," I said. That was the most famous skeleton in the museum. Though it's too bad Toby was wrong. A triceratops would be even more awesome than a stegosaurus.

"Yeah. Whatever. Come on, we can't get off schedule."

"But . . ." It was too late. My friends were lost in the crowds. If I wasn't going to see the dinosaurs with them, I guess it didn't matter whether I saw them now or at 11:37. I sighed and followed Toby into the basement.

"Check it out," he said as we walked through the first exhibit. "I love stingrays."

"That's a skate," I told him. I knew the difference because I'd done a report on them. I was beginning to suspect that for someone who did tons of research, Toby wasn't very good about finding accurate information.

"Sure, whatever. Come on—it's time to swing through the Ancient Artifacts of the Northern Hemisphere. I mapped a shortcut that will save us two minutes."

Toby headed down a hall near the skate tank. He turned a corner, and we found ourselves in a wider hall, lined with display cases. One of the cases was open. There was a cart next to it, with tools and stuff, and some small signs. I guess they were getting ready to work on a display.

"Hey, cool!" Toby walked over to the open case and grabbed two wooden sticks. Each was about a foot long, with scary faces and animals carved into it. Toby waved them around. "Look, I'm a shaman."

"You're a twit," I muttered.

He tapped his own arms with the two sticks, and then his shoulders. "I'm casting a spell on myself."

"Hey, kid! Put those down." A guy came running toward us from the other end of the hall. "They're fragile."

"Sorry." Toby put the sticks back.

I looked at the cart next to the case. According to the signs, Toby had been messing with artifacts of the extinct Zwahari tribe, a nomadic people who'd lived in the Gobi desert three thousand years ago. The case had a wish stick and a curse stick, whatever those were. It also had a medallion of wisdom and a flute of prosperity. Too bad Toby hadn't played with those, instead.

We moved along, keeping right to Toby's stupid schedule, walking through the ancient agriculture exhibits and toward the Hall of World Climates.

I glanced at our schedule as we reached the Amazon rain forest exhibit: 10:37 to 10:57. "Twenty minutes?" I asked. "Isn't that kind of long to stand around getting wet?"

"Hey, the rain forest is huge," Toby said.

"Yeah, the real one is. But this is just . . ." I let it go as Toby slipped through the door.

I followed him into a dark, steamy room filled with gigantic plants. The vegetation grew taller and denser as we moved along the path.

"This is awesome." Toby pushed aside an enormous leaf that blocked our way.

"I guess you're right. The room is pretty big." We'd walked at least a couple hundred yards without any turns.

"I hope they have white-handed gibbons," Toby said. "Those are so cool."

I wrote a report on gibbons last year, too. I'd wanted to do crocodiles, but Gabriel beat me to it. From what I remembered, those gibbons were in the Asian rain forest, not the Amazon. Besides—they weren't going to let wild animals run around loose right where people were walking. But I didn't say anything.

At least, I didn't say anything understandable. But I

did let out a yell when a gibbon flew past us, leaping between the trees.

"There's one," Toby said.

I glanced at my watch. The inside of the glass had steamed up, so I had no idea what time it was. Man, it was warm. I grabbed the bottom of my T-shirt and wiped my face, but the sweat kept flowing. I looked back the way we'd come. "Maybe we should just turn around," I said.

Toby glanced at his watch, then shrugged. "I guess we've been here for a while."

"Yeah. Let's find the exit."

"I think we're lost. We should head for a river. That's the recommended method for finding your way out of a forest. There has to be a river nearby."

"There's no river here. This is just—" I stopped talking as a new sound grew above the scattered drips, chirps, and animal calls that surrounded us.

Water. Running water, over to our left.

We had to leave the path and push through the tangle of plants to reach the riverbank.

It was a big river. A really big river. The air felt cooler by the water—which meant that instead of feeling like I was inside a pot of boiling water, I just felt like I was standing too close to one.

I looked at the map. It didn't show a river. "Toby?"
"What?"

"Don't say anything else until we're out of here, okay?"
"Why?"

I wasn't sure. Maybe I was crazy. But I thought about

the gibbons and the river. Whatever Toby talked about after he'd touched those sticks and cursed himself, we ran into, even if it didn't belong here.

But if I told him what was happening, he might say something crazy, like *Maybe there are still dinosaurs roaming the rain forest.* As cool as it would be to see a living, breathing *Tyranosaurus rex,* I wouldn't want to become a snack for one.

"Just do me a favor. Okay? Don't mention anacondas or jaguars or anything. And definitely no dinosaurs."

"Hey, I guess I can do that. But why would I mention—?"

"Sssshhh." I put my finger to my lips.

Toby nodded, and made a zipping motion across his mouth.

We managed to go five steps in silence.

"Can I just say one thing?"

"I guess." I didn't see how our situation could get all that much worse.

"I don't think there are jaguars here."

"Good."

He looked down the path. "But I'm really scared we'll run into some lions."

"No!" I grabbed his shirt. "I told you not to talk!"

"Oops. Sorry. I won't say anything else."

"That's not good enough. You need to take it back!" I screamed. "Say there aren't any lions in the rain forest. Hurry, before they show up."

He moved his lips, but no words came out. He'd made that happen, too. *I won't say anything else.*

147

Behind me, I heard a sound rise above the roar of the water. It was a different kind of roar. A hungry roar.

I turned and ran, tossing aside the map. I didn't think I'd need it anymore. We were off schedule. Chased by lions. Lost in a huge rain forest. It looked like we were never going to get out of here. At least, not alive.

LAST ONE OUT

Last one out is a rotten egg!" Chuck shouted, pushing his way through the crowd getting off the school bus. Chuck loved being first. He could, when necessary, put up with being in the middle, but he hated being last—at anything. It was Friday. No school until Monday. Last school day of the week was fine. Last of anything else just wouldn't do.

"Movie time," he said, grabbing Freddie's arm. "Sound good?"

"Count me in," Freddie said.

"Me, too," Mark said, joining them.

There were six of them gathered together by the time they headed down the street toward the Shangri-La Theater. Chuck was in the lead, as usual, followed by Mark, Freddie, Lou, George, and Herb. "Anyone know what's showing?" he asked.

"New movie," Freddie told him. "Don't remember the name."

They had the answer in a minute. *"Demons from Below,"* Chuck said, reading the sign. "Sounds good to me." He dashed ahead, getting to the ticket booth first. "Last one in is a rotten egg," he called as he hurried into the theater. He gave his ticket to the woman by the inside door, then walked down the aisle, noticing that there was almost nobody in the place.

He heard the door open and close behind him as the others came in. Chuck sped up, went to the front, and grabbed his favorite seat. In a moment, the rest of the guys had joined him. A moment after that, the movie started.

"There are demons below," a really bad actor Chuck recognized from a dozen other films said as the opening credits rolled.

"Where else would they be," Freddie said. He laughed.

"Ssshhhhh." Chuck smacked him.

"Hey, that hurt," Freddie said.

"Just keep quiet." Even if it was a bad movie, Chuck wanted to hear it.

"I'm getting some soda." Freddie stood and walked up the aisle.

"Sounds good," Lou said. "Me, too." He headed toward the aisle.

"Hey," Mark called after him. "Get me some popcorn." He handed Lou a couple dollars.

"Anyone else want anything?" Lou asked.

"No," Chuck said. He returned his attention to the screen, where a bunch of coal miners were digging deeper than anyone had ever dug before. Another bad actor was warning everyone that they didn't know what lurked in the depths of the Earth.

"Have to hit the bathroom," Herb said. He got up and left.

A minute later, Mark said, "Where's Lou with my popcorn?"

"Why don't you go find out?" Chuck asked, annoyed at the constant chatter.

"I think I will." Mark got up.

Then George stood. "Bathroom," he said. He looked back at Chuck and added, "Last one out is a rotten egg."

"Yeah, right." Chuck heard the door slam shut at the top of the aisle. A moment later, he realized that it had gotten very quiet. There was the sound of the movie, of course, but absolutely no other sounds. He looked around. There was nobody else in the theater. Everyone had left. Chuck thought about following them, but that would make him the last one out. He wasn't about to play that role.

Then he smelled it.

"What the—?" Chuck looked around. It was a familiar smell, but not one he expected in a theater.

Rotten eggs?

The ground at his feet began to crack. A hiss of steam rose from the crumbling concrete. The steam smelled of rotten eggs.

Sulfur?

That was the smell.

A hole opened at Chuck's feet. The smell of sulfur, of brimstone, filled the theater. Chuck started to crawl over his seat, trying to get away from the hole. The row of seats tilted toward the pit. A screech of tearing metal ripped through the air. The seats dropped out from under Chuck just as he rolled over them. He landed on the edge of the pit, his feet dangling over the steaming opening. He got to his knees and started to stand.

A hand grabbed his leg. Not a hand. Chuck looked back. Hands aren't bloodred and rippling with tiny blue and yellow flames.

The claw pulled him down toward the hole.

"First one in," a voice said from below, "is a rotten egg."

For the last time, Chuck was first.

DRAGON AROUND

Princess Emerald strongly suspected she'd been snatched by a dragon. She couldn't tell for sure, since she was dangling below her captor, but the *whoosh whoosh whoosh* of giant wings was a clue. Hawks didn't grow this large. Emerald could barely see the tips of the wings on each downstroke. They seemed to be covered with scales. Her rapid rise above the ground and—egads!—above the clouds, was another clue. She'd always wondered whether clouds looked different from above. If the price of this knowledge was a feature role on a dragon's dinner menu, then she would have preferred to remain in the dark.

"Hello?" Princess Emerald called. As she spoke, she realized she didn't even know whether she was clutched in jaws or talons. All she knew was that something had hooked the back of her gown and lifted her away from the castle courtyard. If she was held in the mouth of the dragon, it would be unwise to start a conversation.

But apparently, that's exactly what she had done. "Hello," the dragon said.

"What, exactly, are your plans?" she asked once she'd assured herself that she wasn't plummeting toward the ground.

"Well, dear Princess," the dragon replied in a deep and somewhat hissing voice, "I plan to take you to my cave. That will draw out every hero in the realm. They'll come to save you, for that is what heroes must do. And I will sear them into crispy pieces with my fire, for that is what a dragon must do."

"How horrible," the princess said with a shudder. She had, of course, been taking shuddering lessons from the royal tutor, along with math, science, alchemy, divination, curtseying, weaving, sewing, fainting, tea sipping, gnome watching, tapestry gazing, curse dodging, and, as she recalled a bit too late, dragon ducking. Thinking back to the moment of her capture, she realized she'd dodged when she should have ducked. Now, thanks to that one slight slip, she was going to be used as hero bait.

"It's not horrible," the dragon said as they passed above the highest of the clouds into the warming rays of the sun. "Is a frog horrible when it eats a fly? Without frogs, the world would be filled with flies. Without flies, frogs would starve. There's a delicate balance to our lives."

"But heroes aren't flies," Princess Emerald said.

"They're worse than flies," the dragon told her. "Flies are just pests. If heroes get out of control, the world would become a terrible place. Those wicked heroes would wipe out all the dragons. Then, in search of more sport, they'd do the same to the trolls and the goblins. Once they wiped out everything else, they would start fighting wars amongst themselves and wiping each other out. In the process, much innocent life would be hurt. Forests would get burned, fields would be trampled, animals would lose their homes, even innocent humans would be harmed."

"Still, there must be a better way."

"There is always a better way," the dragon said. "But it is easier to go along with things the way they are. If you are smart enough to suggest a better way, I'm all ears. Small ears, but all ears."

"I'll think of something." If nothing else, it would take her mind off her current situation.

The dragon tucked his wings against his flanks and dropped sharply toward the side of a mountain. They gained speed at a frightening rate. Just when Emerald thought she would have to scream, the dragon opened his wings again and swooped into a cave.

He landed with the lightness of a whisper, then set the princess gently down.

"Pretty impressive flying, don't you think?"

Emerald, who hadn't regained her breath, just nodded. It wouldn't have mattered if she'd had any breath. What she saw in the cave would have stolen it away. The huge chamber was filled with gold and jewels. There were hills of coins and mountains of pearls. There were treasures of all sorts taken from unfortunate heroes: swords, spears, entire suits of armor, lances, maces, and other weapons of destruction. There were rugs and tapestries and countless yards of beautiful cloth. There was even a small catapult.

"So soon," the dragon said.

"What?" Emerald asked.

"Do you hear that?"

Emerald listened, but she heard nothing.

"Sorry, I forgot that you humans are sadly limited in your senses. Poor things. But I can hear the rumble of the first heroes already. They will arrive in less than an hour. They're coming to save you from the fierce and nasty dragon. Oh dear, oh dear," the dragon said in pretend panic, "whatever shall I do?"

Emerald tried sneaking away, one tiny step at a time, but the dragon stretched out his tail and stopped her. She plopped down onto a pile of sheepskins, feeling terrible about the fate of the heroes. "Is there any way I can talk you out of this?"

"Only if you can find another means of keeping the world in balance."

Emerald put her chin in her hands and kicked her leg in frustration. Her foot struck a small crown that was lying on the floor. It bounced against the wall of the cave and rolled back against her feet. She desperately wanted to find a solution. The problem was that the dragon seemed to be right. Knights really did love a battle, or any kind of contest. She kicked out again. The gold glimmered in the crown as it bounced against the wall. An idea glimmered in her mind.

"Easy on the merchandise," the dragon said.

"I do have an idea," Emerald told the dragon. "But you'll have to trust me." She explained her plan.

The dragon didn't speak for several moments. Instead, he closed his eyes. Emerald was afraid he'd fallen asleep. But, a moment later, he opened his eyes and said, "Try it. But hurry."

Emerald leaped to work. She grabbed a piece of sheepskin and stuffed it with cloth, then tied it with leather strips. It wasn't perfect, but it would have to do. Next came the hard part. "I need to disguise myself," she told the dragon. "They mustn't recognize me."

"Over there, by the silk tapestry," he said. "Armor would be too heavy, but try the chain mail and a helmet."

Emerald slipped into the chain mail, then put on a helmet. It was dark inside, and smelled like the farthest corner of a stable—the one that never really gets a good cleaning. She took the stuffed sheepskin and walked from the cave. At every step, she expected the dragon to grab her and pull her back.

"Good luck," the dragon said.

"Thank you." She headed down the hill. *I'm just in time,* she thought as the first horse and rider burst out of the forest. Within moments, the clearing was filled with heroes. They were already arguing among themselves about who should have the first chance to rescue the princess. Emerald wove her way to the middle of the crowd and put the stuffed sheepskin on the ground.

She kicked it. It sailed through the air and landed near Sir Frothy of Lakeland. He glanced down at the ball. Then he kicked it hard and high. The sheepskin ball bounced twice, then got a solid kick from Prince Yackety of Running Mouth. The ball skittered across the field until it was stopped by Count Bighead of Meemeemee.

Her part done, Emerald returned to the cave. "I hope this works," she said to the dragon.

"It appears to be going as you planned," he replied.

In a short time, the heroes were all kicking the ball. A short time after that, they divided into two teams. Mere moments later, they came up with a set of rules for sheepball. Shortly afterwards, they erected a stadium with bleachers for the crowds that just seemed to show up.

Sheepball!

The heroes had found a new passion.

"Nicely done," the dragon told Emerald as they watched the heroes. "That should keep them happy and occupied for a century or two."

"Thank you. I thought it might work." Down below, Emerald could hear the knights arguing about where to put the refreshment stand.

"Would you like a ride back to the castle?" the dragon

asked. "I suspect I am going to have a large amount of free time on my wings."

"That would be lovely," Emerald said, hopping on the dragon's back.

And off they went.

LOST AND FOUND

Hey, look at this," Dale said when he noticed the white square of folded cloth lying by the side entrance to the mall. "Someone lost a handkerchief."

"Yuck," Kirby said. "Don't touch it."

"No, it's not that kind." Dale bent down and picked up the handkerchief. "See, it's a fancy one." He pointed to the initials that were embroidered in one corner. The letters *HCX*, stitched in dark red thread with lots of fancy loops and swirls, stood out against the bleached whiteness of the cloth.

"What's that mean?" Kirby asked.

"It's someone's name," Dale said.

"Then what's that?" Kirby tapped the corner of the handkerchief.

Dale looked below the initials. In much smaller letters, in the same red thread, he saw *YFFI*. "I don't know."

"Yiffy?" Kirby said. "Yuhfie? Whyfee? How do you think you say it?"

"Who cares? It's not important," Dale said. "But I'll bet we can find the owner. Maybe there's even a reward."

"How are you going to do that?" Kirby asked. "Anybody could have dropped it."

"Easy," Dale said. "The last name begins with an X. There can't be a whole lot of people with those initials. Let's go to my place and check the phone book."

Kirby walked along next to Dale, chanting, "Yiffy, sniffy," for a block and a half before Dale smacked him and told him to stop.

When they reached his house, Dale got the phone book from the drawer in the kitchen. Sure enough, there was less than a page of people with last names beginning with an X. This was going to be even easier than he'd thought.

He ran his finger down the listings. "Here we go. Harold C. Xantini. He lives on Bowie Street. That's not far from here." Dale couldn't help grinning. He felt like one of those detectives he saw on TV shows.

"Are you going to call him?"

"No. Let's surprise him. I don't want to give him a chance to think."

"About what?"

"About my reward." Dale waited for Kirby to say they should share the reward, but Kirby didn't complain. Dale grabbed the handkerchief from the kitchen counter and set out toward Bowie Street.

"Here we go," he said when they got there. "Number one eight three six." Dale paused at the edge of the lawn, wondering if he'd made a mistake. The house looked abandoned.

"I don't think anybody's there," Kirby said.

"Let's knock." Dale went up and tapped on the door.

Before he was ready for it, the door flew open. Dale jumped back.

A man looked out. "Yes?" He was old and small and very wrinkled.

"Mr. Xantini?" Dale asked.

"That's me," the man said.

"Did you lose this?" Dale asked, holding out the handkerchief.

"Oh my!" the man gasped, his face breaking into a grin of delight. "I thought I'd never see it again. It means so much that you brought it to me. Thank you. Thank you."

Dale handed the handkerchief to the man.

"Please, tell me how you found me," the man said. "It must be a miracle." He stepped back and opened the door wider. "A true miracle."

"No big deal," Dale said, shaking his head. "It was easy."

"Yeah," Kirby added. "No problem at all."

"But how?" the man asked.

"I used the phone book," Dale said. "You were the only one in it with those initials."

"Did anyone help you? A parent or a teacher, perhaps?"

"No," Dale said. "I figured it out all by myself."

"So clever. So very clever. You certainly shall be

rewarded. The man reached into his pocket. Then he frowned and walked across the room. "I must have left my wallet over here."

Dale followed him into the house. "Well, it's not really necessary," he said, though he didn't say it very loudly. He wondered what his reward might be. The man had mentioned a wallet—so it would probably be cash.

"We both brought it back," Kirby said.

Dale shot him an angry look.

"And you'll both be rewarded," the man said as he opened a drawer under a small table in the living room. "Such clever boys."

"So, what does *YFFI* stand for?" Dale asked "That's the only part I couldn't figure out."

"You fell for it," the man said, reaching into the drawer.

"What?" Dale asked, not understanding.

"You," the man said, "fell," he added, removing his hand from the drawer, "for," he raised the knife, "it," he finished, leaping forward.

The knife fell. Dale fell. Kirby fell. A drop of blood fell on the handkerchief, ruining it. But the man didn't mind. He had plenty more.

COOTIES

We always passed around cooties in the playground, running, chasing, tagging each other on the shoulder or back and shouting, "Cooties! No returns."

Then the victim would have to find someone else. And so it would go until the bell rang and we hauled ourselves inside to learn more about General Washington and the severe winter at Valley Forge, or how to determine the area of a rectangle. We did other stuff when we went outside, too—kickball, the slide, the seesaws with the really big splinters—but somewhere on that playground, some kid was always looking to pass along the cooties.

I never paid much attention to how it ended until one day when my friend Cecil said, "Who had the cooties last?"

"Huh?" I wasn't sure what he was talking about.

"You know. The cooties. I always pass them on, and I'd bet that you pass them on, 'cause you're a pretty good runner. But someone has to end up with them. Who is it?"

"You're crazy," I said. "It's your parents' fault, too. They should have given you a normal name. But they stuck you with Cecil, and it has driven you over the edge and off the wall."

"Sure, tell me more, Eugene."

I punched him and he shut up. But it got me thinking. What happened to the cooties? I never ended up with them. *Never*. And I guess Cecil never did either or he wouldn't have asked about it. Somebody must have ended up with them. But who?

I thought about it all day long. It was a silly, stupid, unimportant question, but it stuck in my mind like a nail hammered into a coconut. I thought about it so much that I have no idea what my teachers talked about in any of my classes. I carried it home with me and carried it to bed. I probably carried it into my dreams, but I don't remember them.

The next day, when I ran into Cecil on the way to school, I said, "Let's find out what happens to the cooties."

"What?"

"You know. Let's watch, and see who ends up with them."

Cecil shrugged. "Sounds like great fun, Eugene. Then maybe we can watch the flag wave in the breeze for the rest of the afternoon."

I punched him again and we walked along without talking. The morning crept by, inch by inch around the face of the clock. Finally, it was time for recess. As I was walking into the yard, Ricky Moses ran up to me, slapped me on the back, and said, "Cooties. No returns."

I stood for a moment, aware that I had two choices. I could pass them on and watch where they went, or I could keep them. Either way, I would know who had them last. But the second choice seemed like cheating. Somehow, I knew I had to pass the cooties to someone else. It was part of the unwritten rules. I looked around for an easy target. Ishmael Knight was just coming out of the building.

"Cooties," I said, tagging him on the arm.

He reached back toward me. "No returns," I added.

Ishmael said something he shouldn't have, and then raced away to pass the cooties on to the next victim.

I backed up into the covered area by the entrance, where I was unlikely to be tagged, and watched.

Ishmael passed the cooties to Brendan.

Brendan passed them to Carlos, who passed them to Billy, who passed them to Jordel. And so the cooties passed from kid to kid as they ran and played.

"Hey, want to kick it around?" Cecil asked, walking up to me with one of those stupid red balls.

"No, not today." I looked back. Walter was the last one I'd seen get the cooties. But he was just standing there now, talking to Dennis. He must have passed them on.

I said something I shouldn't have.

"What's wrong?" Cecil asked.

I punched him.

The bell rang.

Everyone went back inside.

I did even worse at paying attention that afternoon. Luckily, it wasn't so different from my normal behavior that any of the teachers really noticed.

Where did the cooties go?

The next afternoon, I tried again. But some of the kids went running around the side of the building, fleeing the cootie bearer, and by the time I got there, there was no sign of who had them.

The afternoon after that, I decided I would just hold on to them myself. Somehow, the thought of this made my stomach twitch like I was planning to tell a lie or break a rule.

I tried.

I really tried.

For fifteen minutes, I held off. I was sure I could do it. But then, just minutes before the bell, Cecil ran into me. Without thinking, I tagged him and said, "Cooties. No returns."

I was so angry with myself, I punched him.

He ran off.

The bell rang.

"Do you still have the cooties?" I asked him during our silent-reading period.

"You gonna punch me?"

"Maybe later. Do you still have the cooties?"

"No, I passed them to Joey." Cecil sort of tensed up, as if he expected me to punch him. So I did.

I went looking for Joey. "Hey, do you still have the cooties?" I asked.

He stared at me like I was crazy. "What?"

I repeated the question.

"I passed them on to Mike," he said. "Or maybe it was Dennis. Or Carlos. I don't know. Who cares? It's not important."

Yes, it is. I'd lost the trail again.

There was only one way to find out. The next day, at recess, I climbed up to the third floor. I found an empty classroom and watched the playground.

It was pretty easy to tell what was going on. The kid with the cooties would always stop and look around right after he got tagged. Then he would either sneak up on the next victim or make a quick dash for someone slower.

I checked the clock. Just five minutes to go until the bell. Far across the playground, right where the school property ends, I saw a kid walking in from the woods. I barely caught him out of the corner of my eye, and didn't dare stare directly at him. There was no way I was losing track of the cooties this time.

They went around. They came around. They passed around. With two minutes left, just about every kid had gotten the cooties at least once or twice. "No returns" was only protection against the person you gave it to. It could always come back to you by way of someone else.

The kid from the woods had almost reached the edge the playground. He was wearing a plain brown T-shirt and black jeans.

One minute to go. Cecil had them again. He was looking around. He caught Billy.

Thirty seconds before the bell, Billy passed them to John. John looked all around. There was nobody near him.

Then someone walked up to him.

It was the kid from the woods. John tagged him. I could see John's mouth move, even from way up here. "Cooties. No returns."

The bell rang.

I watched the kid. His head was down. I couldn't see his face.

Everyone streamed back into the school. Everyone but the kid. He turned and headed toward the woods.

I didn't think. I just ran down the stairs so fast, the railing almost burned my hand. I dashed out of the building and ran toward the woods.

I spotted him at the edge of the field.

He was walking.

I was running.

He headed into the woods.

I got to the edge of the woods just in time to see him slip between the trees. I followed.

I tracked him as fast as I could without making too much noise. Ahead, after ten or fifteen minutes, the sounds of his movement suddenly stopped. A moment later, I heard the thunk of a door closing.

I kept going until I saw the shack. The wood was so old, the shack looked like it had grown from the ground.

I raised my hand to knock on the door, but somehow I knew it wasn't required. The door was unlocked. I stepped inside.

The room was almost empty. There was a bed and a small bookcase. That was just about all.

The kid was sitting on the bed, his head down, his hands resting on his legs.

"Tell me," I said.

He looked up. I shivered for a moment. He was a kid, a kid just like me or Cecil or Billy, but unlike any kid I had ever met. He was old. I don't mean old like my grandpa, or like that house on the end of the block that's falling down. I mean old like those statues you see in the history books, or like the pyramids. He was a kid, but I knew he'd been a kid for ages.

"Tell me," I said again.

He shook his head.

"Please?"

He looked away from me. Suddenly, as if he'd been lifted by an invisible force, he stood. Then he dropped to his knees. He held his hands out in front of him, palms facing each other, fingers slightly curled. His whole body started shaking.

I wanted to reach toward him. I wanted to help. I was frozen. His head jerked back. He was screaming, but no sound came from his throat.

Something else came out.

Something dark and small crawled from his mouth. Something thick and wet, like black mucus with a dozen tiny, rippling legs. It slithered down his chin to his chest and lap, then moved across the floor. It ran into a corner, where I lost it in the shadows.

Cooties. No returns.

"Why?" I asked him.

I didn't think he was going to answer. But just as I was about to leave, he spoke. "For you. For all of you."

"Why?" I asked again.

"Because someone has to."

"Does it hurt?"

"I'm used to it." He closed his eyes.

As I reached for the doorknob, the words *no returns* echoed through my mind. I feared the door would be locked. I imagined myself doomed to share in his task or take his place.

The knob turned. The door opened easily. I looked back. He hadn't moved from the floor.

"Is there anything I can do?" I asked.

He shook his head. It was just the barest movement from side to side.

I closed the door and walked back to school.

I never told anyone about him, even though I got in big trouble for cutting class. I never told a soul. Not even Cecil. But I hardly ever punch him anymore.

MY SCIENCE PROJECT

always get good grades with my science projects. And this one was the best of all. I'd left it on the porch last night, in a cardboard box. It wouldn't have to stay in the box for long. I'd built a really cool display case out of Plexiglas and wood in shop class. As soon as I got to school, I'd put my project in the case, and it would look just like an exhibit in a museum. My art teacher, Mr. Duchamp, said he'd help me make a sign.

I was so excited, I headed out early. I'd gotten third place last year with my working model of a medieval drawbridge. I was hoping to do way better this time. But my dreams of first place didn't last long. I was only a block from home when I ran into Barton Musker and his gang.

"Hey, what's in the box?" Barton asked as he stepped in front of me. He was so big, I could feel a change in the gravitational field when he approached.

I shivered, not just from the chill in the morning air, but also from the nearness of a kid who got his kicks from hurting people. "Nothing," I said. Even before the words reached his ears, I flinched at the realization of how he would respond.

"Nothing?" Barton asked. "That's a pretty stupid thing to carry. Let's see what 'nothing' looks like." He reached for the box.

I took a step back. But Fritz Garlans, the second-meanest member of Barton's gang, moved behind me. There was no escape.

"So what is it?" Barton asked again.

"It's . . ." I was having a hard time getting the words out. My throat was clenching and trembling at the same time. ". . . an . . ." I gritted my teeth for a moment, then tried to expel the third word. ". . . ape . . ."

"Ape!" Fritz screamed.

They all started laughing and making monkey sounds. Barton hopped up and down and scratched his sides like a monkey. That was stupid. Monkeys aren't apes. They're simians. Gorillas are apes. And I obviously didn't have an ape in the box. Not even a small one. But there was no way I was going to get all that information out in one sentence.

Barton grabbed my collar. "Last chance. What is it?"

"My . . . science . . . project." Somehow, I managed to squeeze out the words. My voice sounded so small, I'm surprised it didn't die before it reached his ears.

"Great," Barton said. "I needed one. I'll bet a nerd like

you gets perfect grades." He snatched the box from my hands.

I was about to shout something angry—not that it would have done any good—when I heard him say, "Come on, let's go to the club."

Okay—this could get interesting. My fear was replaced by curiosity and anticipation. The club was an old metal shed where Barton and his gang hung out. I think it had been a garage or something a long time ago. It was at the top of a steep hill. With the sun beating down on the roof, the air inside got nice and toasty long before the outside temperature warmed up. I waited while they walked off. As soon as they were a safe distance away, I followed, but moved slowly and carefully. The hill was pretty rocky, and I didn't want to fall and go sliding across the sharp stones.

When I reached the club, I knelt by one of the filthy windows and tried to see inside. I could barely hear them talking.

"Let's see what we have here."

"Some kind of paper thing?"

"Yeah. Weird. Maybe it's a model. Science geeks love to make models."

"Pull it out."

"Looks kind of like a beehive."

Which is exactly what it was. I'd tried to tell Barton it was an apiary, but he'd cut me off after the first syllable. I don't think it would have mattered if I'd gotten all four syllables out. He still wouldn't have known what that meant. Bees are in the Apidae family. A hive is an apiary.

I pressed my ear against the window, but I didn't hear any more talking. I mostly heard screams and crashes until the door flew open and Barton came running out, followed by the rest of his gang. They were swatting at their faces and slapping at their clothes. I winced as I watched them tumble down the hillside and roll across the sharp stones. It looked like beestings might be the least of their problems.

I'd have to wait until evening to get my hive back. The bees wouldn't settle down until it got cool inside the shed. But that was okay. The project wasn't due until tomorrow. And I was pretty sure I wouldn't have to worry about running into Barton or his gang for a while.

THE BLACKER CAT

Here's your first present." Uncle Roderick held out a thin package wrapped in red tissue and tied with a black bow.

"My birthday isn't until tomorrow," I said. I didn't miss the "first present" part, which meant there was more to come, but I felt I should make sure my uncle knew the right date.

"That's why I'm giving this to you tonight. It will prepare you for the real present."

Prepare me? This was getting interesting. I took the package. Uncle Roderick had a strange sense of humor, and no kids of his own. I was his only niece. So some of his presents were weird, but he was always generous. Once in a while, I got something really amazing, like the kid-size electric car he gave me when I was six, or the beautiful snow globe he gave me the year before last.

Of course, the fact that he didn't have kids meant that

he also gave me a present now and then that was too old, too dangerous, or too explosive for a twelve-year-old girl. The object in my hands didn't look like it belonged in any of those categories.

"It feels like a book."

"Perhaps it is," he said.

It was.

I read the title out loud: *"The Black Cat."* The words were printed in gold on the dark brown cover. I ran my fingers over the letters. I could feel the curve of the C in *Cat.* The letters weren't just printed—they were actually stamped. The smell of real leather tickled my nose. Beneath the title was the name Edgar Allan Poe. "I've heard of him. He wrote that poem about the raven."

"And other things. As I mentioned, this is just to prepare you for your real present." He gave me a mysterious smile.

"Then I'll be sure to read it tonight." I definitely wanted to be prepared.

"Speaking of which, off to your room," Mom said. "You're already up past your bedtime."

"I'm almost a year older," I said.

"You're almost a day older," Mom said. "Good night."

I didn't argue. I was actually eager to go to sleep, since it would be my birthday when I woke. I changed into my pajamas, crawled under the covers, and opened the book.

The story was pretty short. It didn't take much time to read. But I didn't fall asleep for a long while, because the story was also horrifying. It totally creeped me out. It was about this guy who does something terrible to his cat. And then the cat tries to get even. It was really not the perfect bedtime tale, and it was definitely an imperfect birthday gift.

Every time I closed my eyes, I saw black cats with glowing yellow eyes. Slitted goat's eyes. Long fangs dripping saliva. Claws clotted with bits of slashed flesh. The cat in the story had only one eye. I didn't even want to think about how he'd lost the other one. I love cats. I love all animals—all living things, really—except for wasps and snakes. But this cat that slinked through my mind was scary.

"Happy birthday," Mom said when I came down to the kitchen the next morning. "Sleep well?"

I shrugged. Birds had started chirping by the time I'd finally drifted off.

She poured a glass of orange juice for me, then got to work on her special blueberry pancake batter. "Uncle Roderick called. He's going to be here at noon with your present."

I hope it's not another story.

While we ate breakfast, Mom gave me my presents, including the ones my other uncles and aunts had sent. I got all sorts of nice stuff—lots of clothes, some gift certificates, and a pretty coral necklace from one of my aunts. But I couldn't get that story out of my mind. As soon as he showed up, I planned to tell Uncle Roderick how inappropriate his gift was.

When the doorbell rang, I raced down the hall. But it

wasn't Uncle Roderick. It was Leslie-Anne Heskith, standing on my porch with her mom right behind her.

Leslie-Anne had a badly wrapped present in her hands and a barely hidden frown on her lips.

"Go ahead," her mom said, giving Leslie-Anne a little push.

"Happy birthday," Leslie-Anne muttered with the same tone of voice a person would use to say, "Drink some poison." She shoved the box at me.

I took it with the enthusiasm of someone who knows she's drinking poison. "Thanks."

Leslie-Anne didn't like me. I didn't like her. She could be real mean to other kids when there weren't any adults around. And she was still angry that I'd gotten the lead role in the play last year. But our moms were friends, so I couldn't always avoid her.

I opened the box. It was a small mirror. That part was fine. But the frame was sort of creepy. It had a guy's face and shoulders carved at the top. The rest of the frame was made of his arms. Leslie-Anne's grandfather owns this shop full of antiques and old junk. I think she does all her birthday shopping there, taking stuff nobody would buy.

"You like mythology, right?" Leslie-Anne said.

"Yeah." That was true. But I was interested in Egypt, Greece, and places like that. This looked—well, it just looked weird.

"It's an ancient snake god," she said.

"I see." I took another look at the arms. Yup—they were snakes. Their heads wrapped around each other at the bottom of the mirror. Great. Just what I'd always wanted. "Uh, thanks."

"You're welcome." Leslie-Anne squirmed free of her mom's grip and scooted away.

I went upstairs and put the mirror on the table next to my bed. I wanted to toss it in a drawer, but I figured Mrs. Heskith would ask to see it the next time she visited my mom.

The doorbell rang again. Uncle Roderick was on the porch, holding my present. I froze, stared, and forgot all my plans to tell him what I felt about that story.

"Happy birthday," he said. "It would have been cruel to wrap him."

I wanted to shout, *For me?* But I was afraid the answer would be no. This all seemed impossible.

He held the cat up. "Go ahead. Take him."

Afraid it was some sort of trick, I reached out and put my hands on either side of the cat. His fur was soft, but I could feel muscle and bone beneath it.

I'd always wanted a cat. But not a black one with fur so dark, it seemed to swallow the sunlight. Not after last night.

"Did you ask Mom?" I said.

He nodded. "Of course. I'd never do something to annoy my sister. She can be quite fond of revenge."

Mom came up behind me and put a hand on my

shoulder. "We did have a bit of a discussion," she said. "But your uncle convinced me that you're old enough to be responsible for a pet."

Uncle Roderick let go and stepped back. I held the cat closer. He wasn't all grown up, but he wasn't quite a kitten, either. He purred and stared up at me with green eyes. Two of them. No slits. No fangs. No flesh on his claws. He didn't seem evil.

"What's wrong?" Uncle Roderick asked. "I thought you'd be floating in mid-air and making little high-pitched squealing sounds."

"Nothing's wrong," I said. "I love him." I bent my head down and rubbed my cheek against the soft black fur. The cat purred even louder and sniffed my ear. "Uh, Uncle Roderick?"

"Yes?"

"Did you read the story before you gave it to me?"

"I think I read it many years ago," he said. "I don't remember most of it. But I wanted to give you a nice hint about your present, and the man in the bookstore told me this was a classic. Why?"

"Nothing." I went back to nuzzling my cat. I also silently forgave my uncle for not paying enough attention to the sort of books he picked for me.

"He needs a name," Uncle Roderick said.

I didn't even have to think about it. "Loki." That seemed perfect. Cats get into mischief, and Loki was the Norse trickster god.

"Good choice," Uncle Roderick said. "But wait! There's

more." He went back to his car to get the food bowl, litter box, scratching post, and other cat-related items he'd stashed in his trunk. It took three trips for him to bring everything inside.

"Happy?" he asked when he was finished.

"Happy," I said. I put Loki down on the couch next to me. He paced around for a moment, then crawled into my lap, kneaded my leg, and fell asleep.

Definitely happy.

"You're not like that cat in the story," I whispered.

Loki's ears twitched, but he didn't wake up.

That night, Loki came upstairs and followed me down the hallway to my bedroom.

"This is where we sleep." I patted the mattress. "Come on, Loki. Come in."

He stared at me from just outside the doorway. Then he hissed. It wasn't a little hiss. His mouth was open so wide, I could see all his teeth. I let out a yelp and backed away. Loki hissed again. The hair on his back bristled and his tail curled under his body. I could almost imagine him leaping on my face and clawing my eyes.

I slammed my door.

The book, *The Black Cat*, was still on the table next to my bed. I picked it up and put it in my drawer. I didn't want to think about evil cats.

All night, I kept waking up. I heard sounds. Faint tapping and scratching. Maybe he was trying to get in. I pulled the covers up as far as they would go, and tried to ignore the sounds.

The next morning, Loki woke me up by purring in my ear. I sat up, startled. I guess Mom had opened the door when she went past.

I looked at him. "No more hissing?"

He licked his paw and groomed his face.

Okay. That's better. I scratched him behind the ear. He closed his eyes and pushed his head against my fingers.

Loki followed me around for most of the day. He also slept a lot, right in a sunny patch that came through the window. I knew cats did that. Even when they're asleep, they look so pretty.

I thought everything was fine. But Loki hissed at me again when I went to bed that night. I slammed the door and tried to calm myself as I got ready to go to sleep.

Loki scratched at the door.

I ignored the sound.

He scratched harder.

My stomach clenched. *I'm the human,* I told myself. *I'm in charge.* I opened the door and stared at him. There was no way I was hiding in my room.

He hissed and took a step toward me. I backed away a step.

He took another step.

"Loki!" I yelled. "Stop that right now!"

I thought about the black cat in the story. I thought about all the evil things that happened. Every scary story I'd ever read tumbled through my mind. Suddenly, I knew I'd made a mistake opening the door. Somehow, this black cat was going to hurt me. Badly. Maybe even kill me.

He was inside the room now. It was too late to try to close the door.

I looked around for something I could hold to protect myself. I couldn't let him get to my eyes. I reached for a pillow.

Loki's hiss turned into a yowling snarl. He leaped straight at my face.

I screamed and ducked. He flew right past my shoulder. I heard a crash.

I spun toward my bedside table. Loki was there, growling. His head was down. He'd knocked the mirror flat and was biting at it.

No. He wasn't biting the mirror. He was biting something that was coming through the glass. Something that wriggled and whipped, trying to escape his jaws.

A snake.

Loki had his teeth locked on its head. He yanked his own head hard, pulling the snake from the mirror. I could see other snakes behind it—dozens more—bumping against the glass like they were trying to come through.

Loki shook the snake. I heard a snap, like a tiny firecracker. He opened his mouth and let the snake fall to the table.

It wasn't like any snake I'd ever seen. It had a head like a wasp, and small barbs along its spine. Its tail forked three ways. One part ended in a rattle. The other two ended in stingers.

Loki batted at the snake. It rolled an inch or two, limp and obviously dead. A motion caught my eye. More snakes had gathered near the surface of the mirror, tapping at the glass, scratching against the surface, trying to push through. Loki batted at the mirror. It fell off the table and broke. No more snakes slithered out.

Loki clamped his jaws around the body of the dead snake and padded out of the room. I picked up the broken pieces of the mirror and put them in my trash can. Then I snapped the frame. The instant I broke it, it crumbled to dust in my hands.

Loki came back ten minutes later. I didn't want to know what he'd done with the body.

"You saved me." I stroked his head and neck as he settled down on my bed.

He purred, as if to say, *No big deal. That's what cats do.*

Yeah. Cats aren't evil. I looked at my drawer, where I'd stashed the book. Then I glanced at the trash basket next to my bed. Nope. I loved books too much to throw one out—even if it was too scary for me.

But I knew exactly what I was going to do with it.

"Guess who has a birthday next week," I told Loki.

I lifted the curtain and looked out the window toward Leslie-Anne's house. "And guess what I'm giving her for a present."

Sweet dreams, Leslie-Anne, I thought as I slipped under my blanket and cuddled with my fabulous, heroic, and not-at-all-evil black cat.

LITTLE GUYS

Check this out," Avery said as he walked into his room. He pointed to the corner opposite his bed. "I got the whole thing last week."

"Cool trains," Jasper said.

"And my grampa just sent me something to add to my set." Avery held up the opened box that he'd unwrapped right before Jasper came over. "It's all in scale. That means everything is the right size, but just shrunk down." He put the model house on the tracks next to the train.

"Can I run it?" Jasper asked.

"After me." Avery threw the switch that powered the train. The locomotive pulled its three cars around the oval track past trees and barns and miniature chickens. Then he pushed the switch the other way, and the train ran backwards.

"My turn?" Jasper asked.

"In a minute." Avery ran the train forward and backwards around the track three more times. He really liked running it, but he knew Jasper would get angry if he didn't share.

He was just about to give Jasper his turn when his friend shouted, "Hey, there's something inside there!"

"What?"

"Look." Jasper pointed at the model house.

"You're crazy." Avery scrunched down and peeked inside. "Wow! You're right!" he shouted when he saw the tiny man. "There's someone there."

"Let me see." Jasper squeezed in next to Avery.

"Don't push." Avery scooted over and made some room for Jasper, but he didn't take his eyes from the window. He spotted several more people in the house.

"Cool," Jasper said. "Hey, I know. Let's put the house on the tracks."

"Yeah, that would be awesome." Avery picked up the house and set it across the tracks right behind the train.

"It's my idea. Can I run the train?" Jasper asked.

"Next time." Avery got the train running at full speed. It shot around the track and smacked into the house. The collision knocked the train off the rails and sent the house tumbling halfway across the room.

"Crash!" Avery said.

"Cool!" Jasper shouted.

Avery picked up the house and looked inside. The people were still in the room, but they were all lying down. They weren't moving.

"Oh man," he said. "I think I broke something inside."

"Will your grampa get you another?" Jasper asked.

"Sure. He sends me stuff all the time. I'll just tell him—"

Avery never finished his sentence. A giant ripping sound tore through the room. The floor tilted at a crazy angle.

"What?" Jasper gasped.

Avery staggered as the house rose into the air. He barely got out of the way of his bed when it slid across the sloping floor and smashed into the wall.

Earthquake? Avery wondered. *Tornado?*

The room had gotten dark. Avery looked out the window. A giant finger lay across the lower half. The finger shifted, and a face appeared.

"Put us down!" Avery shouted. "Please." He kept shouting and begging. But the face, giant as it was, was a face much like his own. His own age. His own smile whenever he thought of something cool to do. The eyes were a different color, and the hair was longer, but that didn't matter. It was a face he knew well. It was a face without mercy.

A CURE FOR THE
UNCOMMON VAMPIRE

People hate me because I'm so much smarter than
they are. It's not just the kids in my class. My
teachers hate me, too. They all want to be the smartest
person in the room. But they can't be that. Not when I'm
around. So they hate me. I don't care.

I'm bored out of my mind in school. I spend the time
thinking up inventions. I've come up with three ways to
end world hunger and two ways to eradicate malaria, but
I haven't shared my ideas. People don't deserve to benefit
from my brilliance. It serves them right for hating me.

I was sitting in science class, listening to Mr. Hackmire talk about photosynthesis, when the best idea I've
ever had hit me. There might be a way to use a similar
chain of chemical reactions to cure vampirism. Nobody
else would ever make the connection. That just shows
how brilliant I am.

I know most people don't believe in vampires. But last

year, I did a study of them, because they intrigue me. I gathered all the information I needed about populations around the world, and wrote a computer program to analyze the data. There was a definite anomaly. Some populations shrank more than they should, as if members were being picked off. And some groups lived far longer than they should, on average, as if certain people were immortal. Or, at least, immortal until you drove a stake into their heart or dragged them into the burning rays of the sun.

Vampires and I have a lot in common. I was born smart. Vampires live for centuries, so they have plenty of time to learn things and become very smart. I don't fit in with other people. Neither do vampires. I don't care what happens to people. Their pain doesn't concern me. I like darkness. The list goes on and on. And now, I knew how to cure the vampires of their affliction. They'd worship me.

By the time Mr. Hackmire finished drawing a shaky picture of a leaf on the board, I'd worked out a complete theory, inspired by photosynthesis, but also drawing on a half-dozen concepts from molecular biology, organic chemistry, and particle physics. I had to force myself not to race out of the room and get started immediately. Luckily, it was Friday, so I could devote the entire weekend to my project.

The instant I got home, I began perfecting my formula. It required a variety of amino acids, as well as several inorganic ingredients and trace amounts of three rare-earth metals. Fortunately, I have a well-stocked lab. My parents didn't disturb me. They learned long ago that it was best to leave me alone when I was busy with a project.

I stayed up all night Friday and worked straight through the next day. By Saturday evening, I had the formula. It was a thick brown liquid, incredibly concentrated. A single drop on the tongue would turn a vampire back into a human. I suspected the transition would be painful, but the pain would only last ten or fifteen minutes. After that short stretch of agony, the vampire could return to a normal life as a human. I rarely smile, but the absolute brilliance of my creation made me grin.

Now I just had to test my solution. I knew beyond any doubt that it would work. But knowing wasn't good enough. I had to see it work. I needed validation.

I still had my vampire studies on my hard drive. I was almost positive there was vampire activity nine miles from here, in Rackham Hills. The actual victims were spread over a wide area, but it was trivial to trace the center of this vampirism back to its source. This was perfect. I could travel to Rackham Hills on my bicycle. I often go for long rides when I want to get away from people.

Sunday afternoon, an hour before sunset, I placed a vial of the cure in my jacket pocket and told my parents I was going out to observe the occlusion of Venus by Jupiter. That was nonsense, of course, but it amused me that they had no clue.

I took back roads to the southern edge of Rackham Hills. The most obvious place for the vampires to hide was an abandoned building. The most obvious building would be one with no windows and a deep basement. Even when protected by a coffin, a vampire wouldn't want to be near sunlight or in a place where he risked being discovered. It had taken me less than five minutes on the Internet to narrow the possibilities down to a single location.

The sun was almost set. I wanted to be there when the vampires rose from their coffins. It would be an amazing sight. I took my flashlight from the bag clipped to my bicycle. I'd given this next part a lot of thought. Any mistake would be terrible. But I was too smart to make mistakes. I put a drop of the formula on each side of my neck. The instant the vampire tried to bite me, the cure would start and he'd be powerless to hurt me.

The building looked like it was falling down, and far too dangerous for anyone to enter. That's exactly what I'd expected. They'd created that impression to discourage visitors. I could tell as I stepped inside that the building was sturdy. The floor felt solid beneath my feet. The entrance to the basement was hidden, but I found that, too.

What I didn't expect was to find a single coffin. Just one, shoved against the far wall. I stood off to the side and watched it. The lid started to rise. I must have drawn in a deep breath, because the lid froze for an instant. He—or she—heard me. They have amazing senses.

They're also fast. I didn't realize how fast until now. The lid flew open. Before it even struck the wall, he was on me—a blur of darkness, a stink of moldy soil.

I was knocked back, but he clung to me. I felt a hot breath against my skin as he thrust his fangs toward my neck. There was no time to think, or even to hope my plan had worked.

The effect of my formula was even faster than the attack. The instant his mouth brushed my neck, he shrieked and fell away, collapsing on the floor and writhing like he'd touched a high-tension line. He rolled across the floor and howled. His arms and legs shot out, flailing in the air.

The screaming continued for eleven minutes and thirteen seconds. I timed it with my watch. And then, as if a switch had been flipped from ON to OFF, he stopped thrashing.

For a moment, he lay still. Then he raised his head and looked up at me. I stood where I was and waited. He could come to me. He staggered to his feet. He was a small man. Maybe two inches taller than I was, and not more than twenty pounds heavier.

He sniffed the air and frowned. He ran a thumbnail across the back of his hand, scratching himself. The scratch didn't heal.

"Human?" he asked.

I nodded. "You're human."

"How?"

I told him. It was nice having a chance to demonstrate my brilliance to someone who had already seen the evidence.

When I was done, he said, "This is a miracle. It is what

we've been waiting for. What we've been hoping to discover for centuries." He reached out and touched my
shoulder. "You'll be known for all of time as the one who
saved us."

I'd expected praise and thanks. But not this much. Still,
he was filled with the wisdom of centuries, and knew I
deserved more thanks than he could possibly give me.

I thought about his words. "You said, 'We've been waiting.' Where are the others?"

"Nearby," the former vampire said. "I don't get along
with them all that well, because I'm so much smarter. But
they'll listen to me now. Let me go ahead to tell them
what you bring. I want to make sure you aren't hurt."

He shifted some boxes, revealing an entrance that led
deeper into the basement, then paused and looked back.
"Do you have any idea what it's like to have to hunt for
all of your food? To have to hide what you do? To live in
constant fear of hunger and discovery?"

"It must be awful," I said.

"It was. But now it won't be, thanks to you. Let me
prepare them for the news." He slipped off.

I put more of the formula on my neck, just in case. I
waited. It didn't take long for him to return. I guess all
the vampires were eager to be human.

"This way," he said.

I entered a room lined with open coffins. A dozen men
and women had gathered in the middle. One of them,
the tallest, said, "We have long hoped for a day like today.
We owe you great thanks."

As I opened my mouth to reply, I realized he wasn't talking to me. He was thanking the one who had led me into the room.

"You are brilliant, Abraham," the tall vampire said. "We chose well when we gave you the task of guarding us." Then he lunged at me. Before I could react, he wrapped his arms around me. I braced myself for the bite. But he just held me there, clutched in a grip so solid, I felt as if a tree had grown around my body. Another vampire walked over and wiped my neck with a cloth.

Then they both bit me.

The transformation into a vampire is long and horrible. The next two hours were wrapped in unbearable pain. When I could finally speak without screaming, I realized I wasn't human anymore. I had changed in a thousand ways. I was still weak from the transition. But I knew what I had become—one of the undead who thirsted for blood.

I sniffed the air and looked across the room. Abraham, the one who had led me here, was also on the floor. I could tell from his lifeless smell that he'd been turned back into a vampire.

I didn't understand. I looked up at the tall one, who was standing above me. "Why did you do this? I brought you a cure."

He smiled. "I know. And we will use it." He lowered himself to his knees and put his mouth near my ear. "Thanks to you, we no longer need to hunt."

He reached out and put a drop of the formula on my

lips. If I thought the pain of becoming a vampire was terrible, the pain of becoming human was ten times worse.

I realized I would experience this agony a hundred times.
A thousand times. I would experience it over and over as
they drank my blood, turning me into a vampire, and then
cured me so they could drink my blood again. And again,
and again.

A WORD OR TWO ABOUT THESE STORIES

The most common question writers are asked is, "Where do you get your ideas?" The answer to that, for the stories in this collection, is given below. Here, as a bonus, are the answers to eight other common questions I get asked when I visit schools: No, I don't live in a mansion. Yes, I plan to write another book. Green. *Ender's Game.* 1954. Yes, I have a gamer's tag. Bacon. Nope, I won't autograph your forehead.

Not Another Word
As faithful Weenies fans know, one of my best sources of inspiration is my what-if file, which has now grown to more than sixty pages. Each day, my first writing task is to write a what-if question, such as "What if a mime was actually . . . ?" (You know the rest, unless you haven't read the story yet. In which case, get out of here. Go read the stories. Then you can come back. I mean it. There are spoilers here.) I suspect a lot of readers would have

been happier if it was the mime who met an unpleasant ending in the story. Maybe next time.

Get Out of Gym for Free

When I was in high school, the gym teacher really did pick four kids to be leaders. I've always remembered that—mostly because I would have gladly done anything to get out of gym. Naturally, given that my best sport was reading, followed closely by eating and wheezing, I didn't have a shot at the position. But the concept stayed with me. And then it hit me that a last-man-standing contest would be perfect for picking a leader. And for making the teacher's life much easier.

Ghost in the Well

Another what-if idea. I started with the idea of a ghost that appears to be asking for help, but is really tricking the helper into joining her. In this case, I knew from the start that the ghost would do something bad to the main character, so the real work was to make this happen in a satisfying way. (Satisfying for the reader, that is. I'm pretty sure the main character would have preferred a different ending.) Manga fans might notice that the title is a pun.

It's Only a Game

Many years ago, a cable service was available that would download games to certain systems. That was one part of the inspiration for this story. I own a fair assortment of video game consoles, but I tend to lag a bit when it comes to keeping up to date. (No need to hold a fund-raiser for me—I finally caught up.) So I've often found myself half a generation behind the rest of the world. It was easy to imagine a kid who was several generations behind. That was the other half I needed. Once I put those halves together, the aliens pretty much had to show up.

Attack of the Vampire Weenies

It hasn't escaped my notice that there are some people who get all giggly about vampires. When people get giggly, it's fun to think of ways that things can turn dark and unpleasant. I'm pretty sure that if you do some research, you'll find it is the vampires themselves who started all these rumors about how attractive they are. We Weenies folks know the truth, and never leave home without a clove of garlic or some werewolf bodyguards.

Rapt Punzel

This was purely inspired by the title. I liked the idea of the girl in the tower being enrapt by something, and television was a natural choice. It's fun and easy to fracture a fairy tale. Try it at home. As for the grisly ending, the stuff that happens in the original versions of many fairy tales makes my stories look positively cheerful.

In One Ear

My ancient earphones have started to disintegrate, trailing bits of foam everywhere. I started looking at new ones, and saw that most of them are inserted into the ears. It's hard not to go from there to thinking about ways that things could turn unpleasant. I also noticed that some people almost never remove their earphones.

Fourth and Inches

This is a pretty common sort of idea. I'm sure we've all imagined that we were suddenly thrust into whatever we were watching. I touched on the concept when I wrote about a remote control with a hidden INSERT button. That story, "We Interrupt This Program," from *The Invasion of the Road Weenies,* was much messier.

MutAnts

This story was totally inspired by the title. Often, a word will turn into a pun or some other form of wordplay in my mind. It wasn't a major stretch to think that a mutant would be an ant that mutates. Or a whole lot of ants. As always, an idea can go in a variety of directions. On a different day, the mutating ants could have caused something funny to happen.

Cat Got Your Nose?

I'm fond of cats, and I'm fond of girl geniuses. The former sometimes smells. I thought it would be fun if the latter tried to find a cure. As a side note, I realized that I've done a bad job of giving dogs equal time in these stories. However, as you've already seen if you've read the stories before reading these notes (and you really should), I've started to make up for it with "Walk the Dog."

The Ride of a Lifetime

Many years ago, I was at Hersheypark with my family and some friends. There was a new coaster I was dying to ride. I got in line, and the sky started to darken. I could see lightning off in the distance. I made it to the ride before the storm closed things down, but the concept of trying to beat the storm lingered with me. Also, I live near Dorney Park, which has a great assortment of rides. Every year or two, they add a coaster or other major thrill ride, and it's always special in some way—the tallest, the fastest, the longest, and so on. So it's not surprising I'd have coasters on the brain.

Chirp

A what-if story. This one was tricky. I don't ever want readers to guess the ending of a story before they get there, but I also want to scatter some clues so the reader can look back and realize that the ending was inevitable. So I had to show the girl's passion for birds while trying to distract the reader from thinking about whether she shared the main character's magic. If I'd been really brave, I would have also given her some catlike traits, but that would really have been a risk, since I know my readers are smarties. I actually read this aloud at several schools and stopped right before the ending to ask the audience to raise their hands if they thought they knew what was going to happen. Enough kids were surprised by the ending that I felt the story would work.

Bruja

The ending came to me first. I loved the potential horror that would happen if a person unleashed that potion in some catacombs. So I had to figure out how to get the characters underground, and how to break the bottle. That's part of the fun of writing stories. There's a lot of problem solving involved. But it's fun to solve this sort of problem. The best part is that there are thousands of solutions. How would you get a girl into the catacombs?

Elf Improvement

I wasn't sure where this one would go when I started. I just liked the idea of some small creature making life miserable for some innocent kid. In the first version, I just had the elf switch its attention from the kid to the teacher. But I realized there had to be some sort of scene that explained why the elf's attention got transferred. That's why I added the scene with the shirt. The nice part about this—and here's a tip for you writers out there—is that the answer to most story problems is already hanging around somewhere in the story.

Sun Damage

I mentioned that I write a what-if question every day. That's only one half of the equation. I often know what I want to write about. But sometimes I get stuck. Then, when I need an idea for a story, I skim through the file until one of the ideas resonates with me. (*Resonate* is a great word. You can make things vibrate if you sing the right note. And ideas can make us vibrate.) In this case, the idea was "What if some vampires gained strength from the sun?" Of course, the idea is just the beginning. From there, I had to think up a situation that would bring this what-if to life. Or to death.

Sweet Soap
I started out writing about a kid who was an inventor. (It seemed fair to balance the girl genius of "Cat Got Your Nose?" with a boy genius in this story.) I'm not sure where the soap-to-candy part came from. But once I got that far, it wasn't hard to figure out the direction the rest of the story would take.

Roadwork
They're constantly fixing roads where I live. And I recently noticed a five-man road crew just standing around, staring at a small pothole. One of them had a shovel, but he wasn't doing much with it. Maybe that's why I had this story in mind. This sort of story, with a fairly simple shock ending, is best kept short. As with "Chirp," the hardest task is to try to keep you from seeing what is going to happen. Though, if you guess the ending, that's okay, because there's pleasure in being right, too.

Finders Losers
There is a faded silver tot-finder sticker on my daughter's bedroom window. The sticker was once bright red. I see it every time I go outside, and I see lots of other stickers

all around the neighborhood. It was natural for me to eventually mold that sight into a story idea.

Cloudy with a Chance of Message

I saw a letter in the clouds a while ago. (I can't remember whether it was a *T*.) It wasn't clear and sharp, like in this story. But it got me thinking about messages in clouds. I'm not sure, in this day of microwave ovens, whether people still use teakettles, but I liked the imagery of the ending, so I kept it in. (This would be a good time to lower the book and tell the nearest adult, "Imagery is an important component of both mainstream and literary short fiction." They will be impressed.) Obviously, this title is also a pun.

Family Time

I used to play a lot of board games. Sometimes, the rules were ridiculous. And I've had people try to teach me various games over the years. Some were a lot of fun. Others just had too much stuff to keep track of. I thought it would be interesting to write about a kid who just doesn't understand the rules. (In case you were wondering, the rules in the story are total nonsense. I had fun making stuff up.) I think all of us feel clueless at times.

Gee! Ography

Yup—another what-if. "What if a kid got all the right answers on a test even though he hadn't studied?" When

I got ready to write that one, I realized a geography bee would be more fun than a test. Often, when looking for the best way to turn an idea into a complete story, I look for something that will allow as much opportunity for dialogue and action as possible. I don't want my characters sitting around and thinking too much.

The Spider Shouter

With everyone whispering to mammals these days (horses, dogs, uncles, whatever), I thought it would be a nice change of pace to have someone communicate with insects. I actually like spiders. Though I'm more than happy to deal with them one at a time.

The Pyramid Man

If you've read the story, you know what a pyramid scheme is. (It's called that because the number of people involved grows larger with each level. One person sells to ten. Those ten sell to one hundred. They sell to one thousand. It expands just like a pyramid, until it runs out of buyers.) It's basically a bad thing. But it hit me that it would be wonderfully amusing to have someone start a pyramid scheme by selling pyramids. What can I say? I'm easily amused. But not easily scammed by pyramid sellers.

Walk the Dog

As a cat owner, I can't help noticing that dog owners are always saying, "I have to go home now and walk the dog." My daughter recently got a dog, so I'm even more aware of this. I liked the idea of a girl who is supposed to walk a dog, but is too busy and selfish to really care. When I told my daughter about the ending of the story, she said it was a good example of irony. (She's not just a dog owner. She's also an English teacher.)

Warm Rain

I touched on this idea in an earlier collection, in a story called "Head of the Class." In that one, I had a kid whose mistakes become truths when his teacher reads his papers. This idea was similar—a kid who is wrong about everything, but turns out to be right. I have this nagging feeling I should have done more with the triceratops, but he really wasn't interested in taking part, so I gave him the day off.

Last One Out

My initial idea was just to write about a kid who hated to be last. At some point, the old saying about rotten eggs entered my mind, which led me to think about the way that old eggs can smell like sulfur, which made me think of other things. It all sort of got mixed together, leading to the painful conclusion.

Dragon Around

I just started writing. I figured, with a dragon carrying a princess through the clouds, something interesting was bound to happen. Happily for her, I wasn't in a dragon-feeding mood that day.

Lost and Found

All of us have stumbled across lost objects. It's our nature to want to return them. Sometimes it's easy to find the owner. Other times, it's impossible. I guess I had that in mind when I came up with the idea that a lost object was actually a trap. The story did present me with an interesting problem. In a traditional monogram, the initial for the last name would be in the center and not on the end. But it would have slowed down the story and taken too long to explain this or have the characters figure it out (thus passing the information to the reader). So I decided it was okay, in this case, to ignore that fact and hope it wouldn't distract very many readers from the story.

Cooties

I was thinking about cooties (I have too much leisure time), and it hit me that someone has to be the last person to have them. I'll have to admit that this story does leave some questions unanswered. We sort of know what the cootie keeper does, and why, but there's still a lot that remains cryptic. It's not that I didn't want to answer those questions. The truth is, I don't know the answers. Maybe I should have dreamed some up, but I liked the ending the way it was. I try not to do that too often. I don't think it's a bad thing once in a while. Hopefully, the pleasure the reader gets from the story itself is enough to justify putting it in the collection, even if I really don't know all the details about the guy in the woods.

My Science Project

I liked the idea of a kid bringing a beehive for a science project. Then it hit me that it would be even more fun if someone stole the hive from him. It took a bit of work to figure out how the thieves could be made to suffer for their actions. But I like thinking about science and nature. One of the joys of writing is that I get to explore all sorts of subjects. (I won't even tell you some of the wonderfully icky research I found myself doing for my Nathan Abercrombie, Accidental Zombie series.)

The Blacker Cat

I thought it would be fun to have an adult give a young lady a copy of Poe's story "The Black Cat" before giving her a cat. In this case, art imitates life. I have to admit I'd forgotten how horrifying the story is. When I went back and reread it, I realized it really wasn't something I'd recommend for a young reader. Which, of course, made it even more interesting to think of some well-meaning uncle giving it to his niece.

Little Guys

I wasn't sure whether to include this story, since I had one somewhat like it a while back ("Bobbing for Dummies"). But I think they're different enough that they can both be allowed to exist. As for the idea, it's from the what-if file.

A Cure for the Uncommon Vampire

I started with the idea, "What if a kid discovered a cure for vampirism?" That idea could have gone in a lot of different directions. But then the twist hit me, and I knew I'd come up with something I really had to write. I try to end each collection with something very scary, and this one felt perfect for that position.

Well, that wraps up another Weenies book. I am both thrilled and amused that I am able to spend so much of my writing time crafting short stories. In past Weenies books, I've thanked pretty much everyone who's helped me. I considered skipping that part this time, since it's mostly the same folks. But ink is cheap, my gratitude runs deep, and some people are invaluable. So, with a minimum of annotation, allow me to offer my thanks to those who've been essential to the Weenies at some or all points throughout the course of these five books: Joelle Lubar, Alison Lubar, Kathleen Doherty, Susan Chang, Jonathan Schmidt, Dot Lin, and Weenie artist Bill Mayer.

Thanks, also, to Weenies fans, both young and old. I am a small part of a large chain. Just as I'd be nowhere without my readers, I could have gone nowhere without the writers whose work fed, and continues to feed, my own imagination throughout my life. Rod Serling, Ray

Bradbury, and Stephen King are at the top of the list, but there are dozens of others who stand tall among those giants. Lastly, big thanks to Joshua Malina for giving me lots to daydream about.

Okay, I'm done. I need to send this book off so I can get started on the next one. Maybe I'll finally figure out a good way to end that unfinished Botox story, or the one with all the scorpion paperweights. As for the half-written one about the five hundred dolls' heads, I may just chicken out and leave it alone.

READER'*f* GUIDE

ABOUT THIS GUIDE

The information, activities, and discussion questions that follow are intended to enhance your reading of *Attack of the Vampire Weenies*. Please feel free to adapt these materials to suit your needs and interests.

WRITING AND RESEARCH ACTIVITIES

I. I Wonder . . .

A. Wondering "what if" is a great way to start a story. For example, one might imagine David Lubar starting the title story of this collection by wondering "What if vampires weren't the handsome, sparkly characters of bestselling fantasy novels?" With friends or classmates, make a list of the "what if" scenarios that might have inspired other stories from the book.

B. Use paper, magazine clippings, computer art, colored pencils, and other craft materials to make a collage of words and images from *Attack of the Vampire Weenies.* Include character names, locations, unusual objects, supernatural creatures, themes, action words, and anything else that catches your attention in the stories.

C. Choose four words from your collage of exercise I.B. above (preferably words inspired by more than one of the stories). Write a "what if" question incorporating those words. Then, write the outline for a short, scary story that answers your question.

D. Several of the stories stem from main characters' selfish or greedy actions. Write a paragraph describing a time in your life when you were jealous, unkind, or misbehaved in another way.

E. Use the paragraph you wrote in exercise I.D. above as the starting point for a scary fictional story beginning with a kid experiencing the same emotion as you did. Include a monster, insect, or other creepy creature—and a bad outcome for the kid!

II. Scary Characters

A. Make a list of the creepy characters found in the stories of the *Vampire Weenies* collection. Then, create a table or pie chart showing how many characters are supernatural, how many are insect-related, and/or other categories of your choice.

B. Choose a favorite creepy character from the book. Sketch a cartoon-style portrait of this character, or write a 2–3 paragraph fictional biography of the character's life before the moment you meet them in the story.

c. With friends or classmates, make a list of scary characters from books, movies, and television. Take a class vote to choose the top five scariest characters. Or paint a class mural featuring frightening faces.

d. Learn more about a scary story writer from the past, such as Edgar Allan Poe ("The Raven") or Mary Shelley (*Frankenstein*). Write a short report on the writer's life and work. If desired, come dressed as that writer to present your report to classmates.

e. Interview friends or classmates to find out whether they like vampires, what they know about these creatures, what books or movies about vampires they have liked or disliked, and what type of vampire stories they'd like to read in the future. Compile your information into a short, newspaper-style report entitled, "What is it about vampires?"

III. Unlucky Outcomes

a. Many of the main characters from the stories in this collection meet bad ends. In the character of one of the story protagonists, write a journal entry that begins, "I wish I hadn't . . ."

b. Characters in the stories show greed, poor judgment, and other unpleasant qualities. Which do you think is the worst quality in a person? Write a paragraph explaining why you think this quality is the worst.

C. Use examples from the story and additional research, if desired, to create an illustrated booklet entitled "Advice for Avoiding Vampires."

D. Use fabric, beads, clay, paper, or other craft materials to make a good luck charm to ward off creepy things. Write a list of instructions for how to use the charm and be sure to explain whether it will work if you behave in a mean way.

E. Imagine you are about to embark on one of the adventures from the story collection. Record a video message explaining what you are about to do and any thoughts you would like to share for friends and family who watch the video.

IV. World of Weenies

A. If you have read more than one Weenie story collection or other books by David Lubar, make a top ten list of Lubar's favorite creepy topics. (Hint: Consider clowns and psychic abilities.)

B. Compare two stories from different books that deal with the same subject from the list. What elements do they share? How do the endings differ? What conclusions might you draw about the subject based on your comparison? What might you like to ask the author about this subject?

C. Design an imaginary website for David Lubar's "Weenie World" including such elements as a biography of the author, a description of each Weenie book, factoids, illustrations, a "Dear Vampire" advice column, or other features you think would work well on the website.

QUESTIONS FOR DISCUSSION

1. Why do you think the author chose "Not Another Word" as the first story for this collection? Consider the personality traits of the narrator, the surprise at the end of the story, and even ways you could interpret the title as you answer this question.

2. Compare the narrators of "Ghost in the Well," "In One Ear," and "Lost and Found." What character traits do they share? How does this inform their actions? Do you see any similarities in the villains of these stories, or the bad outcomes that befall the main characters? What conclusions might you draw from any similarities you observe?

3. In "It's Only a Game," "Fourth and Inches," and "Little Guys," describe the different ways the main characters are unaware of the effect their actions have on others. Do you think the characters should be held responsible for their seemingly careless actions? Do you think human beings sometimes behave this way in relation to their environment or other aspects of the world in which they live? If yes, give an example.

4. The author features vampires in several stories. In what ways does he play with vampire stereotypes or poke fun at vampires in popular books? Describe some

unique qualities of vampires in stories from this collection. Which is your favorite vampire story from this book? What appeals to you about this story?

5. Insects are another recurring image in such stories as "MutAnts" and "The Spider Shouter." Why are insects a creepy or frightening story element? Explain your answer.

6. What supernatural, nonvampire elements are featured in "Bruja," "Elf Improvement," and "Warm Rain"? Do you believe in supernatural creatures? In magic? Do you think your beliefs effect the way you read these stories?

7. Kids in this story collection are not always nice, but some are quite smart. In "Cat Got Your Nose?," "Sweet Soap," "My Science Project," and "A Cure for the Uncommon Vampire," it is cleverness that leads the main characters into trouble. How do the solutions they invent do more harm than good? What kind of warning might you infer from these stories?

8. Several Vampire Weenies stories can be read as commentaries on various news-making problems in today's society. What real-world problems do you think the author is addressing in "Rapt Punzel," "The Pyramid Man," and "Dragon Around"? Do you agree with the points he is making? Why or why not?

9. Do the stories in this collection change the way you think of your own feelings of anger or frustration? Do they reflect any of your own fears about our world? Cite examples from the book in your explanation.

10. On page 189, Avery looks into the face of the giant rocking his world and realizes that "It was a face he knew well. It was a face without mercy." How could you describe this as the organizing theme of the *Vampire Weenies* collection?

David Lubar grew up in Morristown, New Jersey. His books include *Hidden Talents*, an ALA Best Book for Young Adults; *True Talents*; *Flip*, a VOYA Best Science Fiction, Fantasy, and Horror selection; the Weenies short-story collections *In the Land of the Lawn Weenies, Invasion of the Road Weenies, The Curse of the Campfire Weenies*, and *The Battle of the Red Hot Pepper Weenies*; and the Nathan Abercrombie, Accidental Zombie series. He lives in Nazareth, Pennsylvania. You can visit him on the Web at www.davidlubar.com.